Gul Y. Davis was born in 1973. His writing has appeared in various magazines and anthologies, including *Hard Shoulder* from Tindal Street Press. He has won awards from the Royal Literary Fund, the *Financial Times* and the Koestler Awards Trust. He is currently at work on a novel.

A LONE WALK

Gul Y Davis

TINDAL STREET PRESS

First published in 2000 by
Tindal Street Press, 16 Reddings Road,
Moseley, Birmingham B13 8LN
www.tindalstreet.org.uk

A short passage from this book previously appeared in a different
form in the 1998 Koestler Anthology of Award-Winning Prose.

Copy-editing: Joel Lane
Typesetting: James Parsons
Internal illustration: Sally Bonham

ISBN 0 9535895 3 6

Printed and bound in Great Britain by
Biddles Ltd, Woodbridge Park, Guildford.

Dedicated to my Brother and my Ima.

With many thanks for the invaluable assistance
from Vicky Taylor, Joel Lane and the
Swift team of staff.

'. . . and illness hidden
quiet as a stone-fish
as I play
in the shallows.'

One

Dank and dark like it should be, in my bedroom. Clothes strewn across the room; food rotting on a plate by my bed; the curtain on the window closed. Shadows play on the walls, fall like twitching fingers on the cupboard, armchair.

I stick my leg out from the bed, nudge the plate with my big toe. Kick my leg, watch the plate flip. Watch curry soak in its own puddle on the carpet. The potato and string beans lump. Stupid dinner. Sat on the floor since eight – as if things will change if it waits. I sit myself up, put my feet into the warm slop. 'Eat the supper Mother lovingly got you.' I lift my foot, bring it down, hard, in the slop. Feel it splash over my bare foot. I stand, stomping it into the carpet. Stamp it into the carpet. I rub the curry with my foot, a soft sludgy feeling.

I picture Lee's face. His nose broken and mushed. The rest of his face trodden to a broken bloodied pulp. Flecked with blood, I stamp on his broken flesh, feeling it give under my feet.

My throat, muscles tightening. Gagging. Vomit pours down, out of my nose and mouth. Vomit runs, clinging to the bits of hair on my chest, sticking to my open pyjama top. My stomach lets go over the floor. My eyes sting. The stink of curry and sleep. Food in my nostrils, the acid burns, biting the flesh of my insides. I heave again.

Tears run along my cheekbone. I breathe in sharply, closing my eyes, not letting the air escape from my chest. I grin, knock my head back. I holler into the darkness of my room. Listen to my voice bounce around the walls. It will wake Mum. Then she'll be talking to them, telling them. She'll send me back.

ଓଃ

'You're not going to get away with it!'

Lee shoved and tottering, the chair leaned, toppled

back, smacked on the green carpet. Vomit clogged my nose, burning. Sucked to the back of my throat with the gasp I let out as I fell back with the chair, cracked against the floor.

I swallowed it. Sick dripped half-congealed from my face. All tangled with my hair, the smell . . .

I closed my eyes, rested my head back on the floor. Warm and sticky, I let it cover me.

'Get off the floor!' Lee kicked at the upturned chair. The touch of his breath, his face close to mine . . . 'Get off the floor!' His breath turned cold on my cheek. His thumb and fingers dug into my neck, he pulled me up. I kept my eyes shut, didn't take weight on my feet.

'You're getting a replacement meal, Wil – you fucking animal!' He hit me in the stomach. I keeled over in the darkness of my closed eyes. The back of my head hit the wall. Fuzziness. 'You'll eat, Wil.'

Slam. The door's bang echoed across the solitary confinement cell. Lino-covered, with bare stained walls. The sound took time to die. It whispered like forgotten tantrums, until silence ate it.

Is the door locked?

႙

I open my bedroom door. The light of the corridor makes me blink. Crusted tears itch. My feet leaving damp stains on the stairs, I pass the landing bathroom. Turn sharply. Pass the toilet. Climbing the other set of steps to the corridor with doors to the kitchen and lounge. The front door at its end.

Arty pictures, splashes of red paint, squirts of blue on night-black backgrounds. Little metal plates with arty-sounding names tacked to the frames. I smile to myself. See Mum spitting the syllables out from awkward places in her mouth. Her friends nodding their stupid overgrown goatees, saying stupid things back. The wooden owl I carved was much better than all this shit. I look at the hole which used to hold the hook from which it hung. Her Boyfriend has organized everything. Table exactly halfway down the hall. Pictures evenly spaced to the inch. New carpet, nice and soft and pale and bland. Nothing the same. This isn't Mum, all this isn't Mum . . . It's got to be accepted. Can't expect Mum to put everything in the freezer so that if I came back alive and wanted all the old things back, she'd pull them out, defrost them . . . Come on William. Wil, will power, that is me; strong indestructible me. Me.

Not this time. I elbow the mirror behind the table.

Picking up the pen from the table by the vase, I scribble on the Post-It pad: *Mum, gone for a long walk.*

It's too stuffy in here, no air left for me to breathe. I stick the note to the mirror. Breathe out sharply. I stink of sick . . . Opening the front door, I step out. The cold concrete of the steps burns my feet. The wind bites through my pyjamas, under my arms, stings my ears.

It's good to be out here.

Stomp on anything hard, anything sharp, lying on the steps. I tread down to the gate. In this dark the front garden is ghostly. All the flowers and plants; shades of shadow spreading. Half-open mouths drink in the darkness. Shrubs crowd the earth. The ground sucks light in. Has eaten it. Spat out these long alien plants, stiff stems, watchmen of the night. Click. I open the gate, step barefoot out onto the street.

Mum's car. Posh, new, spick, not like the old banger we had, our little dusty Mini, before Mummy's success when she 'made it'. New car, new phones, new clothes, glasses to match the 'Professor' title. Surprised she didn't buy a new up-and-coming home, house. Hampstead, Highgate Hill, or some other trendy lefty, sixties grown up, arty-farty place, with Chinese herbalists, reflexologists, regression-therapists . . .

Cars pack the curving street. Paving slabs. Bloody

cold. My soles full of little imprints from stones, nicks from little bits of glass. I lay my fingers on the bark of each tree I pass as I walk along the pavement. Feel the lumps and grooves. They were young saplings when I touched them last . . .

An old battered Mini, its butt sticking out past the end of the road. A baby chair strapped to its back seat, story books on the shelf and a teddy bear, large pale green eyes. Stupid woman! I make a fist. I smack the window, smack it again, feel my knuckles crunch. The window webs. I punch it through, bloody hand, lodged with glass. I reach in, grab a book, drag it back out through the broken window. More glass splinters. Hugging the book to my heart, I run. I pass the end of our road, something sharp slices underfoot. Can feel the blood stick. A shout. Lights. Mother will wake . . . Turn at Primrose Lane, legs stride.

Dark Durham Lane, I run into the middle of the empty main road, clutching the book, blood running out of my hand. Run, run, run. My heart rattles. No air. Heaving chest. Breathe. Stop. Gasping, I need to rest.

Huddled on the flip-seat under the bus stop, sheltered from the wind whining up the street, tossing cans and crisp packets, pushing them against the kerb. I hug the book, hold the cover against my cheek. *The Little*

Mermaid. Taken from the sea, she had lost her Prince and her watery world. No ease now for the pain breaking across her heart, or the hollow in her chest, or the stone lodged heavy in her throat . . .

I run my fingers across my neck. Finger the slug-like scars.

$$\text{CS}$$

Hold tight, keep still . . . The darkness of sleep merged with the darkness in the room, my dream died like a TV snapped suddenly off. Don't move suddenly . . . My thoughts were loud and awake in my sleepy-sick mind. I slid gently under the strap, a sheet folded into a belt and laid across my chest. Julius, his big black pot-belly heaving, navel stuck out from beneath his jumper, slouched in his seat, the leg of the chair pinning the end of the strap to the floor. On the other side of me, Carl, snoring in his chair, pinned the other end of the folded sheet. Gently does it, here she goes . . . Sleep filled the room, could sense it in the darkness, dreamland had laid its heavy coat over this room. Tonight they would not wake. I knew.

Shuffling on my buttocks, I slipped gently, belly, chest, head, under the strap, got up, stood gently off the

mattress. Mustn't wake them . . . This is it, this is it . . .
I shut the door of my cubicle quietly behind me.

The end of the corridor was spanned by the fire
door. Two windows, dark and shiny.

Crack. I smacked my head on the pane, then again,
I smacked my head again and this time the wired glass
cracked. Glass shattered. I put my fingers through the
broken window and pulled a shard of glass from the
door. Warmth sprang. Blood ran down the palm of my
hand. No good cutting across. Stab deep. Stab deep by the
tendon in my neck . . . I pushed the shard into my throat.
I pulled it out. Comfortable coldness. A blow knocked me
to the ground.

She was screaming but made no noise. Everything
was silent, her hand interfering with mine. Her face
flashed into sight. I shoved her off me. Only one more
stab, I need one more stab! I pressed my hand roughly
against her face, pushing her away. Blood leaked, staining
her face. We rolled. I pushed away her hand. I strained to
lift the blade to my throat again.

'Get off me!' My scream was loud and coarse. Her
hand loosened. I pulled free and stuck the glass back into
my throat.

Her shouting knocked down the walls of concrete
blocking my ears. The alarm sang, wailing, wailing.

'Where are his fucking nurses?'

'In,' heaved, 'in his room.'

Bang. 'They're fucking struggling with each other! You two fuckwits!'

Sleep filled, could sense it in the darkness, dreamland had laid its heavy coat over me. Tonight I wouldn't wake. I knew . . .

ങ

I peer into the gloom that hangs heavy above this empty main road. So soon to be back to dismal greys and blacks . . . Night time and my soul turns inside out. My despair hangs in the air about me, follows me around till the sun rises and the ugly feelings hide back inside my chest, out of view. Night time. Nobody thinks they can see. They could all see me, night time, if they tried. If they wanted to. If they wanted to see what I carry inside . . .

'Wil, you have more insight into your condition than I have known you to have had. I know you are still unhappy. But you are in as stable a state as we are currently able to get you. Your mother is willing to look after you, and frankly, Wil, I would rather that than the other options available to me. You are too young to resign yourself to long-term care. And your mother, I know you feel she is to blame for putting you in the home, but I believe she does care very much what happens to you, give it a chance . . .'

So I must be better.

Better.

I spit the word into my hand and crumple it up like soiled paper. This is better, is it? This is supposed to be me better. I run my fingers across my neck, scratch the scars with my nails . . . Me and Mother standing smiling into the camera; shirt and tie, I rest my head on Mother's shoulder. Chubby-cheeked, a smile, a straight row of white teeth . . . Old Wil Shaw, Mum tries to find him in me now, her sad despondent eyes. If it weren't for Mum he would still be here . . . I would still be him. I shift on the plastic seat of the bus shelter. Goosebumps. Keeping hold of the book in my hand, I stare at the drying blood that criss-crosses my hand, arm. Lodged glass glistens in my skin. Jewels earned by pain.

I finger out a piece of glass. Hook-shaped and see-through. Blood runs from the cut, drips onto the book cover, onto the mermaid sitting on a rock. A trickle of blood cuts the picture in half. Her face smeared red. She cannot see. Sea. Water, deep and cool and calm, heaving in the stillness of the dark. A bridge spans the neck of an estuary, its woven metal glints in the moonlight. The Little Mermaid with long, wet, golden hair beckons me with her seaweed-covered hands . . . Standing on the wall of the bridge, I hear the mer-city call, echoes soothing me under . . .

A bus appears out of the dark. The heavy rumble of the engine. The smell of burnt oil. It heaves to a halt at the bus stop. Two men with cropped hair step down, arm in arm. The small one kisses the one with the beard. They giggle, walk past, down the street. Hear their footsteps on the pavement die into the night . . . Wil the Wanderer, returning to his city after many years in human form. Must meet his mermaid – must find his guide! Be taken to her watery world, or be trapped for ever in this cold concrete land, forever unhappy, never a human . . .

I climb up through the exit doors before they shut, the book clutched to my chest. Warm. Hot air flows through the bus. Empty seats, worn, comfortable and sat on.

'Fare please!' the driver shouts from his cab. 'Next time, don't come in through the exit doors!' I see him watching in the mirror.

I hold up the bloodstained book, let him see the blood running down my arm. 'Fuck you!' I climb the narrow stairs.

Empty, warm. The four-person seat stretches across the back of the bus. Bed . . . With my undamaged hand I grip the handlebar on each seat in turn. The bus pulls away, rumbles down the road. I lie down on the long seat. Sleep . . . Sleep . . .

Two

The policeman blows his nose, puts the tissue in his pocket.

'You awake?' The other officer prods my shoulder.

I open my eyes, sore in the flickering light of the bus. The bus is not moving.

'You fit the description of a person reported missing. Will you come with us?'

I move my hand down to my pyjama trousers, check the flap. Sit up, placing my bare feet on the ribbed bus-floor. I put my palms over my eyes. Darkness again.

'You are not under arrest, but will you come with us?' The policeman blows his nose again. A car screeches past.

'Go away.' I stretch my arms out towards them, holding the book with both hands. 'My mermaid, my mermaid is calling me, I am going to the sea! Leave me alone.' I clutch my book tightly against my chest. Rock myself on the edge of the seat.

'Another nutter.' Rubbing his nose, the one with a cold rolls his eyes, turns to the older policeman.

'Son.' The older policeman steps forward. 'I think you should get that hand seen to. You worried the driver, the bus is stopped outside the police station. Come with me and my colleague,' he looks at the other man, 'and we'll get a few questions out of the way, take you down to the hospital to get your hand seen to.' He pats my shoulder. Looks at my bloody hand. 'They'll take good care of you.'

I clench, squeezing myself to the book. 'Leave me alone! I am not going back!'

○3

Perhaps it was the quietness. An empty feeling that the sounds from the television could not fill. A door shutting, a burst of irritated voices, then there was quiet again. Pictures that chattered moved across the screen as patients drifted along the corridor. The medication shuffle, the manics who drove themselves against the drugs until they dropped, broken. Standing still was the painful thing. It left a residue of time to watch the clocks count the weeks and months; it created a space for the ghosts to haunt, the shadows to shape, the fear to chase. To keep moving was far safer. Pacing the corridor; wandering about the television lounge; sitting in the dormitory; perhaps psychosis was just another place to run, to hide.

Screams; the silence splintered into a thousand sharp pieces. Was she cutting herself or the nurse? The alarm sounded, its noise pumping the air. China fractured; a trolley, knocked over, crashed to the floor, as a sharp push at the fire doors sent staff from the other wards rushing past my door. She cried for help, begged the nurses not to put her in her room.

I blocked my ears. The two nurses in my room did not leave their chairs, they looked towards the door.

Rooms were strange things. If one could come and go, put pictures up, put carpets down, they were a space to call one's own, to enjoy being alone. Lock someone in, then the room became a cell. The walls closed in, the smell stifled, the isolation pained. Doors no longer kept the others out but kept me in; and yes, so easily I could have let myself scream. Scream with the woman out there.

Stretched out, bottom in the corner of his chair, neck tilted, the nurse sat back, looked at the television and listened to the 'goings-on' outside the room. Long brown hair dangled down the back of his neck, oil-stained jeans underlined his statement that he didn't give a shit. That was not a bad thing. He saw these places for what they were: homes for the insane dressed up in words like 'client-centred care' and 'community nursing'. 'Mad fuckers' living on the street and staffing levels that were a 'fuckin' joke'. Red MGs and beer, a much more sensible vocation, he said. Mike worked on his cars and did agency for the cash.

Denis sat next to Mike. Headphones, tiny bits that fitted inside the ear, rested on his shoulders as he listened to the girl banging things against the window of her room. He started to tap his foot. 'Should be fucking shot,' he stated dryly.

I sucked my teeth. 'That will solve a lot, Den,' I said.

'Hitler had the right idea.'

'Wil,' Mike sat himself up, 'take no notice.'

Denis stuck out his little finger. 'I have got you like this, haven't I, Wil?'

The girl had stopped making a noise, the voices in the corridor were drifting off.

Mike was content. He was watching the picture-box's dumb programme. 'I hate *Coronation Street*, Mike,' I said, did not look at Denis.

'All the more reason to get you addicted to it. If you didn't hate it, getting you addicted would be no fun.' He edged himself into a more comfortable position, scratched his chin.

A piece of crockery smashed. No heaving tears or screams, only a groan. I got up, walked to the door. The little nurse was standing on her toes to see through the observation window. An alarm started sounding through the speakers.

'Quickly, quickly!' The little nurse was calling down the hall. Three nurses squeezed out of the office door, ran down the corridor. They barged into the girl's room. Electronic wails kept pounding. I watched the doctor rush down the ward, his bleeper crying.

'Get bandages! Pass me that sheet, apply pressure here!' I could hear something thump. The little nurse hurried out. Hands and shirt covered in blood, the doctor followed her into the corridor.

'Fuck, I should have worn gloves – Paddy,' the doctor directed his voice back into her room, 'I'll get an ambulance, we need to get her to A&E over on the General site.'

'She's bleeding like a fucking pig.'

The doctor looked round, then briskly strutted out of view. 'Where's that nurse?'

Slashed wrists or throat. I knew it. Scars would remind her of the past, years from now. Those walls, they oozed with screams and blood; it got absorbed over their years of standing there, defining the top floor of the psychiatric wing. Cartoons on the TV fell off cliffs into deep canyons. Road Runner was beep-beeping and Coyote was no more than a disappearing wail and a puff of smoke.

Two large ambulance men in green uniforms hurried down the corridor, dragging a stretcher behind them. Her door was opened wide, they squeezed the trolley through; the little nurse was crying. The girl was carried out, her neck and chest covered with blood. Bandages around her throat were soaked dark purple; her eyes rolling back inside her head, she looked dead. The bandages leaked onto the canvas, so her heart must have been pumping. People followed them out of the room. Someone turned off the alarm. Nobody spoke.

I rubbed my neck. I felt the raised scars across my own throat. Coarse hair grew out of the lumpy tissue. Denis looked at me and shook his head. He slipped his earpieces back in and started rocking to his music. It was Led Zeppelin or Queen, something like that.

‍‍

ಚಿ

'I am not going back!' I scream, dropping the book. 'I'm not going back! I am not going back!' Screaming. The muscles of my jaw tear, my eyes roll up. I run at the policeman. He pushes me away.

They grab my arms, pulling them behind my back. I twist round, force my eyes open. 'The mermaid is waiting for me! Need to go, let go of me!' My voice is hoarse and raw. I push my face towards his. Feel my head pounding, sweat running down. I shove the policeman into the metal handle of a seat. He grabs my hair, yanking my head down towards the floor.

ಚಿ

Scrape, the chair slid, toppled back, Derek slammed straight up, table knife in hand, pushed the round dinner table, which shrieked as it scraped across the linoleum floor. Mats, red and yellow squeeze-bottles, salt cellar, pepper landed, staining the floor in a cloud of dust and ketchup. Patients at the other tables lowered forks from mouths, looked round. Derek took the knife to his throat, dug the blunt blade into his neck, drew it down, leaving a deep red mark behind. He looked at the bloodless blade, paused.

'Which one of you is coming with me?'

He cut the knife through the air, the silver caught the fluorescent light. 'Come on! I'll take one of you with me!' His grey beard, flecks of black hair, balding head, creases of concentration on his forehead.

The two male nurses stood still. 'Took a doctor in the Maudsley hostage' must have run through their minds – would mine. I smiled, sat neatly behind a table in the corner of the dining room.

Derek sent his table crashing to the floor. The nurse ran out to the dining-room door, fumbled, fumbled, unlocking the cabinet holding the phone. Stuttered brief words.

'Everybody out!' the other nurse shouted.

Patients, all nineteen of them, drew slowly from their chairs; the lino screeched in a dozen places. Fat Andy started to run, George too.

Brian stopped halfway across the dining room. 'What's the matter, Jack?' he asked, sadness twisting in fidgety hands. His trousers sagged around his bum, the food collected in his lap fell to the floor. Nurse Ann grabbed Brian, tugged, urging him out of the room.

'Who's coming with me?' Derek slashed at his throat again.

He turned round, leaned the knife towards me. His

eyes rolled up in his head, till all that was left was white. He was yelling.

Action-Nurse Noel, athletic, muscles rippling; this was his scene. Pushed past Derek. 'Stand up – now, ya fucker, stand up!' He pulled me from my seat, bundled me from behind the table, dragging me across the dining room.

The nurses were waiting. Dave, Jerry, Andy, Paul, Pete, Ian, Mike, Chris, Simon, Lee. Derek was going to go down, go down hard and fast. I waded through them, trying to avoid Noel's sharp shoves to hurry me up. They plugged the end of the corridor, sweaty testosterone T-shirts bristling outside the doorway.

'I'll take you all fucking with me!' Derek screamed. Through the glass panel at the side of the door, I could just make out Derek waving the knife at them.

'Ann, get a sheet for us, I think that's the best way. I don't want to be cut by the cunt.'

Nurse Ann pushed her way free from the jam, headed towards the linen cupboard. Taking a pile of white sheets, she elbowed her way back through the nurses.

'I'll take one of you fucking with me!'

'All of you, get behind the dinner trolley – Noel, you stand over there, throw the sheet over him!' Dave's voice was deep, words resounded like the vibes knocked from the skin of a drum. 'Noel, you get over there, and at the count of –'

'I'll take you all fucking with me!' The scream from Derek full of futile rage.

'. . . three, two, one!' There was a pause. Silence. Bodies bundled. Derek screamed. Nurses screamed. Someone would end up dead.

ଔ

Their hands pin my arms behind my back, my face crushed against the ribbing of the bus's floor. Heavy boots thud up the stairs. A knee on the back of my neck, sending shooting spasms through my shoulder blades. Handcuffs bite, lock round my wrists. The knee releases its weight. Muffled voices talk around me. They pull me onto my feet, someone grabs my hair, leads me by the head slowly down the stairs. The bus doors suck-slam open, coldness cuts through my pyjamas, stinging, as we go down. I force my eyes open. Paving stones.

It is warm again. I hear the hum of computers, the tap-tap of people typing. Can smell coffee. Keeping me bent double, the policeman pushes me through the room.

Doors crash open, smacking the rubber stoppers on the walls. He eases the pressure on my arms, I keep my eyes screwed tightly shut. Someone slides a bolt, throws a heavy door open. The policeman shunts me forward, I stumble onto a cold floor. My arms tingle, feel blood pumping into my hands. I bring them up before my blurred eyes, watch my hands merge and part and merge again.

Policeman thinks he hurt me, but he is shit, is nothing! I turn, look at him staring at me from the doorway. I push the thumb of my bad hand back, rest it, so it touches, lays flat, soft, against the inside of my forearm. My cuts bleed. I smile at him. Nothing compared with nurse-locks, nothing! My vision clears, blurred edges hardening. I stare back at the policeman in the doorway of the cell.

'Stop fucking around, kid, it's not me you're hurting.' He slams the door shut. The lock turns.

I lie down on the mattress in a corner of the cell, curl up tight, hug myself under the flickering dull light. Rest, I rest in the darkness of my closed eyes . . . I picture a planet covered in brightly lit police cells, every inch of the planet's surface smothered in grey prefab buildings. I sneak up to the window closest to me, it is cold on the planet's surface as I stand outside in between the buildings. I peer in through the window. Inside I see a police sergeant marching up and down in front of a dentist with his hands down the open mouth of a man. It has won, will win, with its bright lights, the fluorescent tubes that beam and burn, will burn in these places long after I am shrivelled up dead and dry . . .

Wiping a stream of snot running from my nose, I flick my hand as the trail of slime sticks to it. I wipe my hand on my pyjamas. More tears run from my eyes, sobs stifle my breath as I cry. I am going to die. I clutch my chest. Sob. Mermaid, mermaid! . . . Mermaid! I stuff my cry into a bottle and fling it into the misty sea swimming through my skull.

Choking on my heaving tears, I wrap my arms about my head, twine my legs.

The cell door swings open. I look up, a frame of light. 'Someone to see you, Wil. Your mother.' The policewoman smiles, beckons me to follow her out into the corridor.

A desk with a tape recorder, the room with a biting light. The door shuts behind me. The video camera up by the ceiling watches, its little focused eye.

Mother. She is crying to herself as she sits at the

far side of the desk, her handbag clutched against her. I feel my skin peel under the harsh light. I walk up to the desk, sit down heavily on a hard plastic seat opposite Mother.

'A week, Wil.' She pauses, stifles a sob. 'A week, Wil. It's only a week since they let you out – look at me.'

I bury my head in my arms, on the desk.

'You,' her tone soft, 'frightened me so, to see your bed empty, and that vomit about the carpet. Why, Wil?' Her hand touches my shoulder, lightly. I cringe, flinch away. 'Not talking to me again?'

'Mrs Shusta.' The interview-room door opens. A soft female voice. 'The psychiatrist is here to see your son. Will you come with me?'

I lift my head from my arms, look round to see Mother walking stiffly to the door, she turns towards me. I bury my head back within my arms, my face presses against my wounded hand. It hurts.

'Your name is William, William Shaw?' The doctor leans forward, resting his arms on the desk.

I nod.

Rubbing his nose, the doctor leans back, suit jacket creasing. 'Do you want to tell me about it?'

I bury my head in my arms, crying.

'You often wander about the streets this time of the morning?' His voice is relaxed. 'Got me out of bed as well, my friend. Do you feel up to talking, because to be honest I am much too tired to know whether I am coming or going, let alone do an assessment – it's an indecent time of the morning, don't you agree?' He rubs his eyes, leans back in his chair. 'I have had a brief chat with your mother, so I have some idea of what's been happening. Given your history of mental illness, it is probably best if I admit you overnight, just to be on the safe side, do this assessment when I am not half asleep, eh?' He yawns, puts the back of his hand over his mouth. 'I work at the Barnet Unit, we have a free emergency bed, a rare event these days.' He picks up his briefcase, lays it in front of him on the desk. He clicks open the locks.

I feel a stream of snot run from my nose, tears well and spill from my eyes. I can see the poison Mum has put into him, see it turning his blue eyes dark and frozen. I am going to be locked away, I am going back . . .

'N, no!' I hear myself scream.

'What are you trying to say, Wil?'

Screwing my eyes together, I block out the interview room, the doctor, the hospital he is going to send me back to. I set iron bars and walls in his way. 'N, no!'

My scream echoing through the deep water of the

sea. The Little Mermaid stops tending to her beautiful seaweed garden, looks about her. I know she can sense something is wrong, I know she can hear me . . .

I am sobbing. The doctor takes my clenched fists in his hands. 'Hush, hush.' His voice is calm. I open my eyes. His bright blue eyes stare at me. 'Hush.' He wipes my face with a handkerchief. 'Your hand looks sore, eh?' He puts the handkerchief in my good hand, walks back behind the desk, sits down, takes a file from his briefcase, starts to write. He rolls the pen between his fingers. 'Let's see if the police are happy to take you to the General tonight – Maslow's hierarchy of needs and all that, best get your physical bits seen to.'

He puts the file back inside the case, shuts the lid. Picking up the briefcase, he stands, walks to the door.

'Doctor,' my voice strained, 'the mermaid is waiting for me. I need to get to the sea. I need her to save me . . .'

He holds open the door. 'Can't she wait until the morning, Wil?'

Three

The sleeves of the coat dangle over my hands. The chatty policewoman leans over the back of the driver's seat, whispers to the policeman driving. She giggles. Stupid schoolgirl . . . The car drives up a hill, past terraced houses with black twisted metal fences. Everything is in shadow, a blood-red sky frames distant tower blocks.

The policewoman plays with one of the driver's sticky-out ears. His neck flushes.

'So, Sarah, what are you doing after work this morning?' He angles the rear-view mirror, grins.

I poke my hand out of the sleeve, push the button

by the ashtray. Whirring. My window lowers, cold air whips around the inside of the car. The policewoman looks at me, sidelong.

'Hang on a second, Phil, I'll shut this window.'

The car slows before a set of traffic lights, the police driver taps the steering wheel with his thumb. In front of the red light, the engine's drone echoes from the empty street. Past the lights, the road falls steeply. The lights turn amber, the driver changes gear.

I reach out of the window, open the door from the outside. The lights change to green as the door swings open, the car lurches forward. I fall out of the car, hands splaying before me. Tarmac rushes towards me. My skull cracks. Pick myself up, pick myself up . . . I force my hands and legs to move, dizzy. I scramble up, start to run down a side road. Hear the police car reversing.

Housing estates, large concrete blocks, either side in darkness, not a spark of light in the square windows. 'One, two.' I count to myself, pacing my running, feet sticky sore on the pavement.

The road slopes; in the distance, a bridge crosses over the road. 'One, two.' I keep running.

An orange sleeping bag sticks out from under the bridge. My feet ache, ache . . . I slow down, stop beneath the bridge. Struggling to breathe, I feel my sweat, damp and sticky in the police coat. My breath sounds hollow.

Three men lie under the arch, against the wall. Cast in shadow, the man in the sleeping bag, curled up, snores. The others lean against the wall. Beer cans rattle about, caught by sharp gusts of wind.

At the far side, an old man sits on the pavement, staring up at the sky. A dirty yellow umbrella lies across his lap. His back straight, he watches the dawn. He turns, staring at me with his wide, pale eyes.

I walk under the bridge, towards him. My feet swollen and sore, my breath steaming in the cold. My head throbs. I feel the graze, wet and sticky beneath my hair. I walk past the sleeping men, snores echoing through the arch. I sit down on the edge of the pavement, next to the old man with the umbrella. I look towards the spreading colours, the smouldering tall glass towers of the city.

I look at the yellow umbrella resting across his lap. He turns suddenly, the umbrella falls from his knees to the road.

'Good morning, Jack. Good morning for it, Jack, don't you say?' He smiles, showing yellow, rotten teeth. His breath smells. He salutes quickly, his voice high-pitched, rushed. He reaches out, gnarled fingers touching me. I flinch away, shrink into the police coat. 'It is bloody cold though – time of year, time of year, Jack. Look at those reds!' He stretches out his arm, points towards the sky, the sleeves of his coat sliding up his wrist. 'A deep red like that, that is as red as the fires of Hell, my friend. Looks hot as fire, hot as fire, doesn't it?' He puts down his arm, stares at me, his pale wide eyes. 'But it is as cold as ice, isn't it, my friend?' Squinting, folds of skin close round his eyes. He peers at me. 'Those long corridors, full of radiators, long corridors of radiators, but it was so cold in those corridors, with all those radiators beaming cold heat – like that sun over there freezing my bones.' He gestures again towards the sun, low in the burning sky. I shift my weight. The man leans forward. 'And the tea, all in a pot, sugar, milk, the lot, in a pot, warmed your belly as your feet froze. Sugar, my friend, hated it, but that's the way it came. That's the way it came.'

○ß

'Do it again, go on.'

Brian loped from one foot to another, swinging his arm round in a bowling motion, the lights in his eyes bright for the second when the ball, if it were there, left his hand and charged, spinning, at the stumps.

Ash, butts, food fell from his jumper. Trousers sagging, the split of his bottom showed, his elastic red underwear. 'I am a good boy, Jack.' He wiped the worn folds of his face. 'I scored three goals against St Andrew's School for Boys – that's a hat-trick, isn't it?'

Sniggers. Brian peered round at the nurses sat about on the tatty armchairs, watched them smirk and nudge each other. His trousers slipped another notch. 'I'm a good boy, Jack.' He yanked his trousers up. They fell to his hips again.

'Do it again, Brian, show Ann how you bowl!'

A small female nurse, bleached blond pony-tail bobbing, walked through the doorframe into the day area. She held a 'staff' mug that steamed into the smoke-filled day room. Ann leaned against the wall near the others.

'I am a good boy, aren't I, Jack?' He looked at Noel, who gave him a thin smile, half-hidden by his ginger-brown moustache.

'You are a good boy, Brian.'

Brian mimed his bowling skills again. In his mind, a demonstration of his former glory; in theirs, a freak performing for their fancy. Like in Victorian days. Anger wrapped itself around my insides and squeezed tight as they laughed at him. School bullies. A crowd laughing at lepers because their own skin was untainted by disease. Easy to laugh in a pack at a man who had lost his own teeth, couldn't bite back. Ann took a slurp of coffee.

Brian tried to kill himself when he was young. He was sixty now, admitted in the nineteen-fifties. They gave him ECT but he tried to kill himself again. I could still vaguely make out the scar on his neck between folds of loose, almost jaundiced skin. Lobotomies were the in thing, so they gave him one. I could see the drill scars too, by his temples. Now he vomited over himself, couldn't stop talking, repeated school memories over and over again – all that was left of his dignity his upper-class accent and the occasional parcel in the post until his dad died two months ago.

'I am a big boy now, aren't I, Jack?' He slapped Noel on the back, raised his voice, dentures dislodging. 'I am a big boy.'

'Brian.' Knocking Brian's hand off his shoulder, Noel raised his eyes so he was looking Brian full in the face. 'What's the rules about touching?'

'I'm to keep my hands to myself, I'm a good boy, Jack.' He twined his hands together as if trying to make himself small, slide out of view, as he turned to go.

'Give me a token, Brian.'

'I'll change my jumper, I am a good boy.'

'Brian.' Noel's lips curled to a smile, a real smile this time, not a placating one to get his toy to play. 'Give me a token.'

Ann stood by the locked door leading to the bedrooms and the dormitories. Brian looked towards the games room. Noel was standing in the way. Brian glanced at the other staff sitting about, his gaze came to rest on Archie slowly folding the newspaper. He glanced at me sitting on the floor. Gwen spread her obese thighs, farted. The stink wafted around.

'But I won't get a cigarette, damn you, Jack!' He backed away from Noel.

Cock fighting, staff crowded round, stood in their lopsided, lazy stances. The day room's scarred armchairs bled yellow foam, the ripped poster on the wall they hadn't bothered to take down.

'Give me a token, Brian.'

His face went grey. 'If you take my token, Jack, they won't give me a damn cigarette!' Brian stuffed his hand firmly into his trouser pocket.

Noel gripped Brian's wrist.

'That's two tokens, Brian – give me them,' he squeezed, 'before it's three tokens and you lose your fag.'

'I am a good boy.'

I could see it coming. Next hour, he wouldn't understand why he couldn't have his cigarette. Brian would try to explain that he had his tokens until 'some damn silly nurse' stole them from him, and that he wanted his 'cigarette, Jack!' Anger would blossom when he was told he couldn't have one without four tokens, and he would ask in desperation and confusion why they took them 'away then, damn it, Jack!'

They brain-damaged him, now they were trying to teach the damaged matter that it was wrong to 'inappropriately touch' or to 'constantly talk when others were asking him to be quiet'. Dragged away to the time out room, he would bang and shout in the darkness against the cell door, still not understanding why they were locking him in, why they were doing this to him.

I didn't either.

Tokens exchanged hands. He called to Andrew in the games room, who would tell him to 'fuck off' when he started to pester on about his school football skills when he was at St Andrew's School for Boys.

Derek had sat calmly through it all. Though I expect, having taken the doctor hostage, this was little to him. An itch at the bit that tells us right from wrong.

&

The old man, his hair white against the red sky, his mouth opening and closing, saying something in a rush. I am a good boy, Jack. Brian's voice echoes through my head.

'Brian, are you Brian?' I stand up, stare at the old man, his white hair, wide pale eyes, duffel coat – he looks nothing like Brian. Brian was completely bald. The man stares back, snatches his umbrella from the road, swings it at me.

I am a good boy, Jack, I scored three goals against St Andrew's School for Boys – that's a hat-trick, isn't it?

'Brian!' I stand up, my chest tightens. I step backwards, reaching into the air behind me. 'Brian?'

The old man's mouth is shouting. He waves the umbrella at me.

I am a good boy, Jack . . . The hairs on my shoulders prickle. 'Is it you?' I look at the old man, reach forward, touch his duffel coat. Coarse, damp. 'Is it you? It doesn't, doesn't look like you.' He knocks my hand from his shoulder, his face angry, raps the umbrella hard against my side.

'Don't hit me!' I cover my face with my arms.

'You're mad too, aren't you, mate?' Pokes at me with the umbrella. 'On your way, Jack, you're annoying me – on your way, go on, go home!' He turns away.

I hear rustling, the man unzipping his sleeping bag. The men are standing up, in the shadows.

Tears well. I put my hands to my ears. *The Little Mermaid, The Little Mermaid,* I left my book on the bus! Her picture, watching me from the sea. I left her on the bus! I run past the old man, away from the bridge. Sore feet slamming down again and again on the road.

'One, two.' I count, pacing myself. 'One, two.' The road curves, I run along the edge of the pavement, past bollards blocking alleyways between the buildings. My breathing a long strained wheeze. I dodge a parked car. I suck air into my lungs, throat burning.

A car is driving up behind me. I stop, turn. A police car slows, its headlights dull in the half-light, its door thrown open. 'Get the fuck back in the car! Now!'

Four

Clean and neat, bandages held with a safety pin. I look at my bandaged hand, wrapped from fingers to forearm. I wiggle my thumb, its nail cleaned of crusted blood. My feet in bandages to the shins. I tap the floor of the car with my stupid foam slippers.

The policewoman and policeman sit either side of me. Scratching his trousers, the policeman looks out of the window. We turn off the road and up a drive, tyres crunch through gravel. A red-bricked bungalow, its glass doors glinting in the sun. Big flowerpots full of white bushy flowers, either side of the double doors. A sign on a post, standing in the gravel: 'The Barnet Unit'.

I look out to the side, green lawn with benches. Two kids sit on a bench, chatting to each other. I watch them as the car rolls to a stop. The engine dies. The boy has a long fringe, brushes the hair from his eyes. Dressed and sensible, they both look normal. Lawns, buildings, benches; this is a newly built, mod-con nut house. I am in the system again . . . Staring at the police car, the two kids on the bench stop talking. The driver opens his door, gets out. I should stay in here, out of the way. Don't want them to see, see me. He unlocks one of the back doors, it rocks on its hinge as it falls back wide. Leaning forward, the boy with the fringe peers into the car.

The policeman climbs out, turns round.

'Time to get out, Wil, we're here.'

I edge along the back seat, my feet sticking out of the doorway. No, the kids can see me . . . Shame wells inside, bloating me, full and sick. I look down at the gravel. They don't fool me, another five years before they let me out again . . . An ache spreads up my chest, taking away my breath. I stop moving.

The policeman crouches. 'Come on, Wil.'

'Come on, Wil.' He reaches into the car.

*

My foam slippers crunch on the ground, the police-woman holds my good hand, leads me through the open glass doors.

A semi-circular reception desk, comfortable green seats set along the walls. Magazines lie open on stained coffee tables. A poster with words in every language is stuck to the side of the desk. Looking up from the computer screen, a woman with a mop of curly ginger hair stops typing.

'Dr Wilson, he's expecting Wil Shaw.' She lifts a book from under the desk, hands it to the policeman. 'I'll phone through now. Sign here.' She smiles.

The receptionist looks at me. 'Up to seeing the doctor, Wil?'

I stare at the floor.

'Do you want me to take your coat?'

Backing away, I hug myself.

'Okay, but you might be hot, it's stuffy in the offices.'

The policeman and the policewoman stay by the desk as I follow the receptionist down a beige corridor with doors on either side.

The doctor from the police station stands in an open doorway.

His forehead creases. 'Good to see you, Wil.'

I walk in. He closes the door, points to two chairs in the middle of the room. 'Come and sit down.' His tone is strong. He sits down, yawns. 'Did you get any sleep, Wil?'

I shuffle over to the seat opposite him, sit down, hang my head.

'Do you have any thoughts on what is wrong at the moment?'

I stare at my bandaged feet in the foam slippers. What's wrong? Tears run, spill down my face. Clenching my fists, I rub my eyes. What's wrong, what has been wrong for so long . . .

'I, I hurt very much.' My throat is dry.

The doctor smiles. He looks sad. He gets up, straightens his jacket and goes to the door, closing it gently behind him. I look around the office, at the desk by the window, the pile of papers, the framed photo of a woman and a child, flowers and green trees blurred behind them.

The door opens. He walks back in, a paper cup in his hand. 'Here.' Handing me the cup, he sits down. 'I guess you haven't had anything to eat or drink, or any sleep, since I saw you last night? How's your hand?' He looks at my bandaged hand. 'I hear you've been running about the streets in your pyjamas. Were you not cold?'

I gulp down the water, feel it dribble, curling under my chin. I wipe my mouth with the back of my hand, stare at the floor. 'When I am cold I know that I am here.'

He leans forward. 'What do you mean?'

'I get so lost . . .' I look at him. 'I don't know what is happening.' He has bright blue mermaid eyes. I wonder if she has sent him . . .

'What do you think is happening?'

'Like I'm dead and my whole life is running all the time before my eyes, I don't know what is real any more, Doctor, so many people crowd my mind that I know have gone.' I sniff, suck back the snot starting to run from my nose.

His forehead creases. 'Your mother says you were discharged last week after ten years in care.'

I put my head in my hands, my palms warm and sticky, I take the weight of my head. The mermaid, she would know what to do. She would talk, I would just follow. The mermaid would take me the rest of the way, take me down deep beneath the sea. I would be free . . . The doctor will trick me, trick me back into a hospital . . . I shouldn't be talking, the mermaid would say I shouldn't be talking! Not to doctors . . .

I stand up, walk to the door, put my hand on the handle, turn round. 'I'm going now.'

'Would you like me to see if I can arrange a bath, some warm clothes and a few hours of sleep, before you set off?'

The tub is bright. I wave my hand under the water, making ripples. Warmness seeps in, easing the tension from my thighs, shoulders. My bandaged feet are propped either side of the tap, my bandaged hand rests on the tub-side. I sink my head underwater. Echoes. My heart beats, pulsing, thumping within my ears. Listen . . .

଼

Sam slid down off the bath's edge, his bottom hit the bathwater: a storm in a teacup, water battered up the bath sides, splashing over onto the floor. My brother, giggling, his blue-grey eyes full of delight, excitement. He batted the water with his hands, splashing about the ducks and clockwork swimmer-frog. His young face creased, he grabbed the turtle bucket, dunking it.

'Oh no.' I laughed. I backed into my end of the bath, hunched my knees, ducked my head behind them, waving him away with my arms. 'Don't splash me again – I'll turn to stone! Go away, go away!'

He stood up. Pulling up the bucket, he waded

through the bathwater, emptied the bucket over my head. I stretched my mouth in opposite ways, gawped like a fish, then shook my hair.

'Ohhhhh, noooooo!' The pitch of my voice went so high I started to choke.

My brother fell back in the bath, laughing.

'Again, again!' He was back up on his feet. Before I had wiped the water from my eyes, there was another downpour. 'Oohhhh, nooooo!' I put my arms round my head, then let go and stuck my neck forward, shook my head from side to side, very fast. 'I'll go hide, hide.'

More water poured.

I sat up in the bath, spat a stream of water from my mouth, put on my half-drowned expression. Sam was giggling again.

ભ

I smile. A forgotten twitch of my lips, natural, smooth. It's been a long time between smiles. I feel the smile on my face, soak it in. It took a lot to shrivel smiles dead deep inside my chest, it took lots . . .

I sink down into the bath, careful that my band-aged feet don't slip from either side of the taps into the water. My nostrils widen, suck air in, push air out. I feel the warm water lap over my eyelids, over the seal of my closed mouth. My bad hand rests out on the edge of the bath, goose-bumping in the cold air of the room.

To be in the mer-city . . . In the darkness of my closed eyes, blue dots double, until all I see is blue ocean. Warm, lulling, full of breasted mermaids singing beautiful strands of song . . . With my good hand I touch my penis, soft and shrivelled and dead. I finger my coarse pubes. My father's face drifts into my mind. His face floats about the dark blue before me, I see him taking off his glasses, wetting the lenses with his spit, wiping them with a cloth. I sit up, out of the water, open my eyes. My feet slip into the water.

ଓଃ

'How does a man wash his hair?'

Father stood up in the bath, hairy body dark and damp, he reached out for the shower-head.

'A man leans his head forward – he's not scared of soap getting into his eyes. Only women lean their heads back!'

I tilted my sud-soapy head forward and the sharp streams of water hit my hair, soap ran down the front of my face, into my eyes. Kept them closed tight.

'That's it, clean, no need to wash again, women worry about hair.'

I rubbed my eyes, looked up, watched Father stand above me, soaping and rinsing his hair. Clean. The soap suds ran down his matted body, trickled down his legs into the bath. He sat down in the bathwater, legs splayed either side of me.

I looked at his feet, then at his dangly-bit, poking just above the surface.

'If you need a pee,' I reached forward, splashing away the suds in the water around his dangly-bit, looked at his, put my hand on mine, 'and you need to have sperm at the same time – what comes first, Daddy? Does the pee come first?' I scratched my scalp, itchy from the shampoo. 'Or the sperm?'

My father twisted his wet goatee beard between his fingers. 'Hmmm.'

Father thought for a long time. I picked up my toy deep-sea-diver man, who lay on the bottom of the tub, played in the dirty bathwater as deep-sea-diver man searched under the ocean looking for the giant squid.

'Sperm,' Dad said, nodded his head. He smiled, pleased with the answer.

'Why?'

'Because.'

'Because isn't a reason, Daddy.'

'Not everything has a reason, Wil.' He slid down in the bath, his dangly-bit swishing about as it grew hard.

Dad sat up, looked at me.

'You will enjoy masturbating very much. Do you know how to masturbate?'

I let go of the toy diver. It sank to the bottom of the bath. 'Why?'

'Because you will need to know these things, it is very important.'

'Why is it important?'

He nodded his head, twisted his goatee beard between his fingers. 'Because.'

'Because isn't a reason, Daddy.'

He carried on like I had not spoken.

'You put your right hand around your penis, you see it all floppy?' He put his hand round his dangly-bit, wrapped his fingers round its trunk. I copied him, fumbling for my bit.

'Then you rub up.' Dad slid his hand up. 'Then you rub down.'

I stopped, stared at his thing growing. He kept on. My hands fell away from my dangly-bit. His grew, straight and true, as he rubbed up and down, up and down. He stopped suddenly, flushed. 'Then, if you keep doing that, sperm ejects.' His voice, slightly broken.

'What does sperm look like, Dad?'

'White.'

I reached my hand forward, wondering if I wanted to touch his thing poking out of the water. I scratched my scalp. My wet hair was still full of soap. 'White what?'

'White,' Dad said again. 'Sticky, holding millions of sperm.'

I opened my mouth, shut it. Scratched my nose where the water itched. 'Show me, Dad.'

He started to rub again. Up, down, up, down. The skin on his thing stretched smooth and tight, its head pointing at an angle to the ceiling, veins down its sides sticking out, blue and purple. He stopped, cheeks red, breathing heavy. 'I will stop now, Wil.'

'Why, Daddy?' I leaned forward, staring at his thing.

'Because.'

'Because isn't a reason.'

'Embarrassed.' He sank under the water of the bath, his knees bent to let his body beneath the water. I moved out of his way.

ଓଃ

The bathwater twists, twists, sucks water down the quarters of the plughole. Water gone where? The sewer – rats and maggots and frogs and snakes that've escaped, grown fat, long in the stench. I hope Father's rotting in a snake's belly . . .

The bath, metallic, digging against my bones. Water's washed away . . . You will never have to watch, to see, you cause pain then walk away . . . What would Mum do, if she knew, knew why you left us?

'Why did I never make a better choice of a father for you? But I suppose if I had, you wouldn't be you.' I lean forward in the bath, resting my head on my knees. Mum, do you wish you hadn't had, had me – a different Dad, could have had a healthy son? Saved from all this pain, more time to get work done . . . A graduate Wil, another success to notch on your board of clever achievements . . . Failed on husband, failed on son – feel so sorry for you, Mum . . . I am crying. I smack my head hard against the tiled wall. I listen to my head sing. The dampness of the empty tub soaking into my bandages.

Mermaid, where are you? Sobbing, I shudder in the empty bath.

The bathroom door clicks open. A fat face, brown, pokes around the door.

'You okay in there, Wil?' Six foot bursts through the doorway, big belly covered by T-shirt. I close my eyes.

'My name's Wakanini, but everybody here calls me Big Mo.' He shuts the door behind him. 'Let's get you outta that thing – they're no good if they're not hot and warm and wet and waiting to be laid in to soak away stress.'

He throws a towel, it falls across my legs. 'You'll get sore, sitting in that empty thing.'

Big Mo, crouched down, rests his arms on the rim of the bath. Smiling. His eyes remind me of the sea, the sea is calling . . . A merman in disguise, come to rescue me? His broad face, grinning. Don't be stupid! Bastards, all of them! I bite my tongue, blood. Taste. I turn away, looking at the wall.

His eyes, grey, looking calmly down into my soul . . . I screw my eyes shut. I still see him, looking calmly at me, in the darkness of my closed eyes. My anger cools. Sleep, I want to sleep . . .

'Watch ya feet.' He offers his arm for me to lean on. I climb out, lowering my soggy dressings onto the lino floor. 'I'll get those dressings changed for you, once we got ya dressed.'

I stand naked, wet bandaged hand, feet. I wrap the towel round my waist, hold it in place. Sigh. Big Mo puts his hand on my shoulder. 'You forgot how to smile? Come on, I'll show you to your room.' I follow him out of the bathroom, down a carpeted corridor, past numbered doors. 'You get some rest. You got pyjamas?' We turn the corner. A girl with bandaged wrists walks past. 'Do you mind wearing hospital issue?'

I stop, back away to the wall.

'Stuff pyjamas – sleep in the nude, most men do. Come on, your room's just here.' Big Mo hands me a key, points. I walk to the door. 'Your room, Wil. Go in, get under the covers, get some sleep, best thing you can do. The linen's fresh.' I look at his grey eyes, broad face, straight-set teeth, his smile not stapled on. I unlock the door, shut it behind me.

CB

I have longed for this darkness, so rare on an adult psychiatric ward. To lie down and shut my eyes, no fluorescent bulb pounding blood-red through my closed lids. Seventeen was my age, and the place such a contrast to the brightly painted cartoon characters that tried to cheer the walls on the children's wards.

I began to pray. Three was a holy number, a nurse once told me. I took three deep breaths, counted each carefully, I must not draw in six times. Each day I looked into the mirror and saw three sixes reflected in my eyes. Satan was there, stabbing at my heart, making me bleed.

'Dear God, grant me a healing sleep. I pray that tomorrow I am not so alone inside; that my pain is numbed, that my world is kind, that I am not tormented, Amen.'

I wiped my eyes. Men should not cry but the tears kept coming. The man in the bed next to me was talking to the night. He had summoned his dead son and his face stared so intently that, for him, his son must have been there.

My home was now an old cloth where the embroidered stitches had faded to the same bland colour as the material it was stitched to. I tried to decipher the image: I saw the colours of my room at home, blue skirting board leading to white wallpaper covered in peeling certificates from swimming and school; magic stones in a plastic case at the back of my desk; magic books tall and proud on the mantelpiece by my unmade bed. Those books . . . They were my treasures, found on library shelves: stories with a child who discovered he wasn't trapped in an unhappy life, but could fly through time to places far away that others could not see.

School playtime in the library, avoiding the playground where bullies' promises were kept. Sometimes, sat at the back of the bus on my way back from school, my bag ripped, my work crumpled, I knew inside me that any second now, time would freeze. That I would walk through the motionless pack of passengers out onto the road, which would be covered with snow. A tall man, waiting there, would tell me I had powers and that I was special and that I had to save the world from darkness – then the kids would not matter any more, my father would not matter any more. I was special, I was powerful, I knew I didn't need them any more. I was an Old One now.

I remembered watching from the rooftops, London spread out like a map, falling into insignificance as the orange ball of fire set, silhouetted the tower blocks. My island underneath the bridge where I sat with Annie, too shy to speak, listened to her talk of her father and the mask called Ann she wore at school and the works of Shakespeare that lined her shelf because they looked good and intellectual.

The bullies never made me cry, I would look up to the sky and lose myself in dreams where the heavens were blue and the clouds were white dragons flying, carrying the Lost Boys on their backs.

The embroidered tapestry was better faded . . .

I looked around the room, at the dark shapes. Perhaps if I imagined hard I could paint an earth road winding in front of me, two climbing mountains peaked with snow, a hobbit, a princess, beckoning me to climb out of bed and step into their world . . . Ravenous, I fed in this place where I was starving. What would nourish me when, consumed, those pretty cakes were gone?

My mother visited me. I spoke to her, but no words left my mouth. She touched me and asked me again, for her sake, to say her name. I beat my head against the ice wall that encased me behind the pupils of my eyes. I wanted the ice to break so I could climb out, into her arms. I stared at her in silence.

Lead weights; the demons bore down. Alone hurt. I watched the dark shape of my belt, hanging over the side of my locker. I remembered the tightness against my throat, the black haze that turned into shades of grey, from the light of a faraway window. I seemed to be walking towards it, and as I neared, I could make out green fields and a little boy running down through the long grass, clothes streaming like royal robes. The Wanderer returned to reclaim his realm . . .

The man had stopped talking to himself, I heard the sound of heavy breathing through his clogged nose. I rested my head on the pillow and shut my eyes. Awake, I listened to the stirrings of the sleeping patients. The silence here was peaceful and warm. I liked night time, nobody talked or asked questions, pronouncing their arrogant syllables as they told me I must speak. They did not understand. I had lost my words and time would never freeze to save me.

ଔ

The curtain on the window open, daylight let in. Shadows flicker on the walls, the built-in cupboard, the locker by the bed. Grey sky fills the windowpane. I lie awake, watching the specks of rain flit against the glass.

My heart beats, a steady thud in the quiet. The rush of distant traffic. A kid shouting. An alarm sounding, somewhere far away. The blue carpet, beige walls; there is nothing of mine in this room. A stained locker with someone's stickers stuck to its top. Two have been peeled off, circles of glue and paper. Nameless room, nameless face. In the system again . . .

I cuddle under the sheet, hug the pillow against my chest, sink my face into it. Cradle the pillow, a baby. Mum cradling me, cradle me . . .

Tap, tap. The bedroom door opens. I turn, lifting

my head. A metal trolley is pushed through, its wheels rattling. On the lower shelf, a mug steams next to a plate with sausages, mash, bright green peas. A white sealed package and bandages on the top.

A nurse with a bob of blond hair. 'Hi.'

A squeaky voice, friendly. Long, rosy face sticking out of a black polo-neck top, a stud in her nose. She smiles.

'You going to let me look at your dressings? Mo says they need changing.'

I roll onto my back, pull the covers up to my chin. She pushes the trolley against the wall, sits jean-bottomed on the edge of the bed. She untucks the sheet, pulls it up over my feet. She looks at the damp dressings, half-unravelled.

'Okay, let's have a look at your feet.' She pulls a pair of rubber gloves from her jeans pocket, stretches them over her hands. They snap around her wrist. She rolls away the rest of the damp bandages.

Blood-leaking scabs, disturbed as the bandages come off. She looks at the sore soles. 'Have you been running through a minefield?' She reaches out, pulls the trolley across to her, unwraps the sealed white packaging, spreading its wrapper out. 'Hmph.' She tosses her head.

She tears a sachet open, squeezes it into a plastic pot. With a pair of green tweezers, she picks up a cotton wool ball, dips it in the pot. 'Lift up your foot.' She grasps the big toe of my foot, pulls it back, washes the bleeding scabs, holds the cotton wool with the tweezers and rubs it in the cuts. She drops the ball on the paper wrapper, picks up another, wets it, wipes the wounds on my feet again. She lifts my other foot, stretches the big toe back, wipes and cleans.

'Now your hand. If we get this done quickly your dinner won't go cold. By the way, you're not,' she frowns, 'Jewish, or Muslim, or vegetarian? I brought sausages, is that okay?'

I nod, pull my bad hand in its damp bandages from under the bedclothes.

In my foam slippers, I tread cautiously out of the bedroom, gripping my towelling dressing gown. Hospital pyjama trousers, the pyjama top buttoned up. The corridor is a mush of sound: closed doors with music squeezing out through the cracks, a different tune from each room. I turn the corner as a nurse hurries past, pushes open a door, disappears into an office.

I look in through the open doorway of a big, bright room. A settee by the far yellow wall, four patients slouching in sofa-chairs pulled up in front of a telly. Turning the pages of her magazine, a girl with a gaunt face, bandaged wrists, sits next to a nurse.

A high-pitched, hysterical voice. '. . . but how is he?'

Mother's here. I step back out through the doorway, looking down the corridor. A nurse opens a door opposite. I see Mother in the office behind her.

'Wil, it's your mother, she has come to visit, is that okay?' The nurse with the blond bob and the stud in her nose smiles at me.

I look down, the carpet beneath me a deep, cool blue. The sea roars, filling my ears with the crash of waves and the drowned sound of a sunken world. The mermaid is waiting for me . . . I turn away, walk down the corridor towards my room. Turning the corner, back into the mishmash of music. My foam slippers pat pathetically on the carpet.

'Wil.' I hear my mother walking up behind me.

My feet freeze, blocks of lead-ice, I stop. Move!

'Wil, why did you run off?' Her disappointed voice. Emotion oozes down the corridor, sticking round my feet, filling me with guilt. I turn slowly around, look at Mum. Her curly grey hair, taut chin, big dark eyes staring out from behind her glasses. She sucks her top lip. 'I have been worried sick. Worried sick, Wil, do you know that?'

'Miss Shusta?' The nurse walks up behind us.

Ignoring her, Mum puts her hand on my shoulder. Her fingers dig gently in.

'Let's go to your room.'

My blood drains, avoiding her hand, leaving my shoulder numb and cold under the towelling of my dressing gown. We walk slowly to my room. I open the door to my unmade bed with flecks of blood on the sheets.

'Have you been hurting yourself again?' She shuts the door behind us.

I shake my head.

'What are those bandages about then, Wil? What on earth is going on?'

Stepping forwards, I rest my hand on the window-pane, look out onto the grey sky.

'How am I going to explain to Ann about her broken car window? There is already so much stigma around our close for you to have to deal with – without you making matters worse.'

A seagull coasts in the air outside. Trees, with drying leaves, hide all but the roofs of the houses on the far side of the green.

'As far as they're concerned, it's criminal damage.

Do you understand? You are breaking into people's cars!'
I look around at her. Her face is taut as she sucks her
top lip. She shakes her head, looks to the floor. I have
hurt her . . .

'Do you want me to take you home, Wil?'

I look at her dark eyes, large behind her glasses. I
lose myself in them, imagine a hug, warm and soft,
Mum's hug . . . Age, we have grown brittle with age. If she
hugged me now, we would snap like two dead sticks . . .
Stay here? Stay in the system by my own choosing? The
mermaid would go mad with rage . . . Go home . . . Stay in
my bedroom, skin dying layer by layer as I lie in that bed.
Watching mother grow more and more disappointed . . .

Tap, tap. The nurse opens the door. 'Excuse me,
Miss Shusta.' She steps inside, closing the door. 'Wil, we
would like you to attend the community meeting. I know
your mother is here, but it isn't visiting time and it was
not pre-arranged with staff, and we expect patients, while
they are on the ward, to participate fully in all group ther-
apies.' She blushes. She turns to Mum. 'I am sorry, Miss
Shusta, we did try to speak to you about this, but you left
the office.'

'Wil, do you want to go to that community meeting
and for me to leave?'

I feel myself crying.

ɔ

'I have a statement to make.' Dad nodded, twisting his
goatee beard between his fingers.

Dr Fenton, Mrs Simons and Vicky sat, a line of three,
before the flat black pane of the one-way glass. They were
watching. I looked at the camera in the corner, up by the
ceiling of the interview room. It was still.

Vicky tapped her thumbs as they rested on her
thighs. Mrs Simons was watching Dad. Silence gathered,
waiting. Mrs Simons' dirty blond hair curled down the
sides of her face. Her shrewd, intense eyes; I saw them trying to work out, guess, what Dad was thinking. There was
no point. He always said what he wanted and, expected or
not, it would hit you where you were bare, naked. It would
hurt. Dad made Vicky nervous, I could see by her twitching thumbs. Mum's face was turned to the window, looking out onto the road and trees. She did not want to hear.

'My life,' Dad's voice was grave, politician-like, like
well-oiled wheels, 'is split into two parts – work and sex.'
He paused, looking around. 'And everything in my life has
to fit into one of them.' He looked around again and then
stared at Vicky.

I held the arms of my wheelchair, brought in
between Mum and Dad. The nurses and doctors kept calling them Mr and Mrs Shaw. My mum got so cross; cross

and red and flustered. And she would shout that she was divorced from this man. They would say 'We apologize, Miss Shusta', say that it was not deliberate, and carry on like it was not a big deal, which would itch under her skin.

Mrs Simons cleared her throat. She cupped her hands neatly on her lap, looked at Dad. The people behind the one-way glass were staring so hard I could feel it. The little motor in the video camera hummed. 'And what part does your son fit into, Mr Shaw?'

Father took off his gold-rimmed spectacles, held them with both hands. He leaned forward. 'My sex life, Wil fits into my sex life.'

૨૩

The nurse puts her free hand on her hip. 'Wil should really attend the meeting. Perhaps you can come back a bit later?'

'Well, I think he should have the choice.' Mum sucks her top lip. 'I have had quite enough. Wil has decided to come back home, as Dr Martins, his consultant at Barnslow, advised.'

'I understand, Miss Shusta, but while he is still a patient here he should really participate in ward activities, that's the point of him being here.' She smiles at

Mother politely. 'Perhaps we should continue this discussion in the office?'

'I live two hours' drive away. Driving through the city on a Thursday is an absolute nightmare. I want some time with my son.' Mum's eyes cut into me. 'Tell the nurse whether or not you want to attend the meeting, Wil.'

I look at the nurse, I look at Mum.

'Wil, do you want to be with me, or go to the meeting? It's no use crying.'

'I want to be with my . . . I want to be with my mother, a little while.'

Mother opens the drawer of the locker. 'Could I have a tissue for my son?' The blonde nurse looks at me: deep blue eyes, the mermaid calling from inside her . . .

Five

Big Mo peers round the door. 'Is Mum gone?' He walks into my room, sits his large bottom on the edge of my bed. His black pony-tail dangles.

My knees tucked against my chest, I lean my head against the wall, sitting on top of the unmade bed.

'You okay in that dressing gown for the rest of the evening, or do you want some of the clothes your mother left ya?'

I look away. Big Mo smiles, shaking his head gently. 'We've had a little meeting in the office.' He scratches his neck. I look away. 'Two things to mention, one important, one minor.' He glances down. 'We don't want your mum to visit for the next few days.'

'I am not staying here a few days.' I spit my words out, don't look at him.

'That's the deal while you are here. Anyway, to the more important point: Clare, the nurse who changed your bandages –' He pushes himself back, resting his shoulders against the wall, a broad grin across his face. 'She said you were cute. Now I said to her she wasn't your sort, that as a man with impeccable taste you would be into rock chicks, as any man after a decent chick is.' Big Mo strums the air. 'Now tell me I am right!'

I try to kill my smile, look away.

'Okay, okay.' He shuffles to get comfortable on the edge of the bed. 'Tell me, what sort of chicks are you into?' He raises his thick black eyebrows. 'I have got to know.'

I chuckle, a smile breaking out across my face.

ଔ

It was my last walk with Nikki before she went back to London and university. She was not like them, Nikki wasn't. She was not crude or rude. She was polite, never looked for an argument. She had a friendly smile, a laugh that lifted, thick lips, a straight set of white teeth. Nikki was nice. With her long mane of blond hair, hourglass figure, the men liked her.

Didn't understand sex myself.

Everybody talked about it, but it did not make sense to me. To get all excited about sticking a piece of meat into somebody else. It was crass.

A doctor appeared two weeks before. The nurses took me into the clinical room. The doctor was waiting by the examination table. He got me to take my jeans down, too big for me, they crumpled to my knees. He pulled my underwear down, felt my balls with probing fingers. They thought I was too asexual for a boy of sixteen. Jabbing into my vein with a needle, he took blood, carried on poking and prodding me, not saying one word.

My silent embarrassment burned in that clinic room. If he had spoken to me, I would have told him that I had been getting strange feelings I had not had before. Strange feelings when I was around Nikki, a nursing assistant two years older than me doing summer work here.

A two-year age gap between us, yet we were worlds apart. She was doing a degree. I was doing decay. She was wise to the world, I could not picture streets or houses or buses any more.

Nikki had big brown eyes. She wanted to design theatres and direct plays. She had a soft feel and smell, like tree sap and long wild grass.

I turned my nose up at Nikki the other day, when she said the best thing in her life was 'jumping bones'.

'Jumping bones?' I asked, not understanding. She smiled, tossed her blond hair and said 'Sex, it means to have sex.' She looked thoughtful. 'I don't like the word fuck or shag, but I think saying jumping bones puts it really nicely, sounds sexy.' Nikki sucked her thumb, looked at me. 'Sex, it's the most wonderful feeling in the world, Wil.'

I thought Nikki had seen it like I did, that I was not alone in my views – I knew, like me, she did not like crude talk. After she said that 'jumping bones' thing I felt like crying, did not know why but it felt like she was one of them too. Part of the same thing as those beer-gutted, sex-self-obsessed men. Nigel, Barry – Rob with his beer-breath and his eight pints a night, who spent the morning shouting out about how he couldn't get it up with that 'fit bitch'. Was there anybody who felt the way I did? Who saw it like me? A turn-off, a shoving of bits of meat in and out, in situations they couldn't picture? Even Nikki, I didn't want to have sex with her, no, sticking bits of meat into other people was not for me.

But to kiss, what was it to kiss, to touch someone else's lips gently with my own? Every time I was with her, something in me dared me to ask, to ask her to kiss. Something stopped me. An uncomfortable feeling I knew had to do with sex being rammed down my throat by my father.

Paul was waiting, holding the door open. Beyond was a gravel drive, then the green lawns and trees of the grounds. On that walk, on that day, I would ask her to kiss me. I had been building up the courage to ask her.

Nikki's blond hair hung down her back, it was tangled because this was the early morning shift, she had not given her hairbrush much use. She wore a baggy denim sweatshirt that overlapped her skirt, and black Doc Martens shoes that exposed her ankles.

'Nikki.' Paul cleared his throat. 'I want the agency nurse to come with you.' His rusty fringe cut a straight line along his brow. His pale blue eyes blinked rapidly as he talked.

The agency nurse put down the newspaper, looked up. 'What is it? Where is it you want me to go?'

Nikki and I walked out into the gravel drive, the agency nurse followed. Cars bordered the two brick walls, gravel crunched under our feet, Nikki held my hand. I let the feel of Nikki's hand on mine consume me.

The other week, a swarm of wasps hovered over the parked cars out here for a whole day. All the nurses were too scared to go to their cars parked in the drive, afraid that this time they would be the ones stung.

Usually conversation flowed like a spring, Nikki talked and I listened, learning about art and theatre and her brother, her mother, and the 'big' world waiting out there. Today was silent, only the noise of our shoes as we followed the curving road bordered on one side by grass, on the other by a building of old dirty bricks. Workmen carried piles of roofing slate, red and white tape marking off the site. The roof looked naked without its plated armour.

The agency nurse, who was humming to himself, hands clasped behind his back, drifted off across the road, distracted by the builders and the cement mixer churning. Nikki stopped walking. Turning, she looked into my eyes.

'You take care, Wil, you hear me – you're going to get better.' Her fingers tightened round my hand, spreading out, reaching under my palm.

I looked about me, at the lawn to the side of us, at our four feet standing still on the paving stones. The sun burned slowly and my cheeks flushed. Suddenly I was filled with hopelessness, a rumble in my belly, a dying groan.

'Nikki . . .'

'Yes, Wil?'

I looked at her moist, cherry-red lips and wanted, with a yearning knot of anxiety, to kiss.

'Nikki . . .'

Tony walked from the cement mixer and the piles of slate, leaned against a parked car, watching us.

'I'll miss you bad.' I turned my head away. Realizing that we were standing still, we started to walk slowly along the pavement. Her hand held mine, her fingers still spread under my palm. I entwined my fingers with hers. 'Write, Nikki, write.' Tears streamed, following the cheekbones, dripped from my chin.

&

'Go on then, laugh!' I tighten my face, lean my head against the wall, drawing my arms to my chest. 'Strum your imaginary guitar because that's what it is – imaginary!'

'Hey.' Mo's smile goes. 'Where did that come from?'

Go on, try! Try to lull me, all this talk of girls – bullshit to try and get me to stay here! Bullshit . . . I feel Nikki holding my hand, her fingers sending a tingling feeling as they rest against my palm. 'You don't understand, I know, I know the way things go . . .'

The way things always go, always have, always will. I know. I don't believe in hope any more . . . The mermaid, a line of drying blood down the cover of the book . . . I wipe the blood away. Polish the picture of the mermaid waving to me from the ocean until it glows in the darkness. Her long golden hair, her arm reaching out, beckoning to take me, take me under the sea. Tears running down her cheeks, she turns to go, dives under, her fin flips out of the water, then she disappears . . . No!

I feel an arm on my shoulder. I heave into the darkness of my hands as I sob.

Hot chocolate, steaming. I draw its smell up my nose, shutting my eyes. I take a sip. Soothing soft chocolate melts down my throat. The quiet hum of the TV.

'If I have ever seen an example of a slimy sucking up, it's you, kiss arse. The only reason she doesn't fancy me is because women don't like bald men.' A patient scratches his chin, moves his queen across the chessboard.

Raising his eyebrows, the other patient moves a pawn. 'It works, Clive, Hannah gave me the hydraulic bed, she understands how difficult back pain can make things – you know she sat on the edge of my bed, Clive, she knows what she's doing wearing that low-cut top, Clive, I am sure she does.'

I watch them from the sofa, sitting on the floor either side of the chessboard.

'Like I said, Ray, if sucking up was a profession you'd have a plunger stuck in your mouth and shit on your nose.'

I shut my eyes again, feeling the warmth of the hot air drifting from the heaters, the sound of canned laughter from the TV, someone chomping with their mouth open. Putting the cup to my lips, I sip hot chocolate. 'Roseanne, how could you?' More canned laughter from the TV.

My eyes flick open as a man in an armchair in front of the TV puts a crisp packet to his mouth, tipping the crumbs out.

A tall skinny man with no hair and a waistcoat strides into the day room, throwing his arms angrily in the air. He's muttering: no words, only an angry babble, as he argues with himself.

Ray grins. 'You are only jealous, Clive, because she fancies me.' He squints. His hand hovers over the board, he moves a rook.

Throwing his crisp packet on the floor, the fat man in the armchair farts loudly.

'Frank, for fuck's sake, you stinky bastard!' Clive glares at him. 'I've got to get out this place, Ray.' Clive shakes his bald head.

Taking another sip of chocolate, I look down into the lap of my dressing gown. Feel the heat of the mug warming my fingers. I am in the system again, the mermaid would shout at me to make me remember, she would say I should get out while I still can, before they suck me in and erase my mind . . . I shouldn't be talking, not to nurses, doctors – be twenty-three in five years' time when they decide to spit me out again. To where? To Mum. I don't want to go home . . .

'Hello.' A girl, I look at her sucked-in face, yellow skin stretched from bone to bone. She sits down on the floor in front of me, crossing her legs, then hugs her bandaged arms, looks away to the TV. 'You are new, aren't you?'

Her grey eyes, sunk deep into her face, framed by her long auburn hair. Her white T-shirt, her arms sticks of bone. A vein pulses by the knuckle in her hand as she holds it against her chest.

I pull my bandaged hand inside the sleeve of my dressing gown. Don't look at my feet, please don't look at my feet . . .

'My name, it's Alison, I just thought I'd say.' Her eyes stay fixed on the TV.

'Wil.' My voice comes out too deep. 'Wil, my name is Wil Shaw.'

I offer my good hand. She tilts her head, smiles nervously, places her bony fingers in mine. We shake hands. She looks back at the TV. An awkward silence.

'Wil, why are you in here?'

I stare down at my lap.

She shuffles uncomfortably, recrosses her legs. 'I am sorry, should have thought maybe you wouldn't want to talk about it.'

It is awkward sitting higher than her, feel like a lord with a servant at my feet . . . I slide down, sit next to her on the floor, my feet sticking straight out in front of me, my back resting against the settee.

A nurse peers around the door of the day room, smiles at us, walks away again.

'Was he looking at you or me, Alison?'

'Me.'

'I see.' I pull my knees to my chest. I look at my foam slippers, bandaged feet. 'Have you been here long?'

'Six months.' Her voice is heavy. 'I should not be here, I suffer from epilepsy, but I upset the doctor on the neurological ward and he sent me here. Mum and Dad don't want me to come home yet, they said that if I had one of my epileptic attacks they wouldn't be able to cope.'

ɞ

Mary had people who loved her. One of the few. I looked at her presents splashed around her on the floor: one, two, three, four, five, six, seven, eight, nine – and her cards too, in their envelopes. Father Christmas and teddy bear wrapping paper covering the parcels. She sat on the floor, presents all around her, her long brown hair tied back in a pony-tail with a blue furry band keeping it together. She picked up an envelope, tore it open, pulled out a pink card. Lowering her head, she sat cross-legged in the middle of all her Christmas gifts, in the middle of the stale, tatty day area. A few decorations hung limply down to the floor, unstuck from the ceiling. Other decorations, looped sticky-paper, crayon drawings of Santa Claus, paper lanterns, looked out of place hanging from these cigarette-stained walls.

I had never seen anyone have a fit before. The other day Mary keeled over on the row of sofa-seats pushed together, relentlessly her body shook and shook and shook. Her eyes rolled back behind her eyelids. I shouted for help.

The nurses came from the office. Four of them. Then Andy walked through into the day area with a pencil behind his ear. He gestured with his short stocky arm, stepped forward and grabbed her twitching ankle. He pulled off her shoe and her sock, then took the pencil, ran the point of the pencil down the middle of her sole. 'She's not faking.' Shaking his head, he let go of her foot. He left the others to attend to her.

Once her shaking stopped, they undid the buttons on her trousers. Andy stood in the doorway, watching from beneath his mop of black hair. Pete, Sally and Nikki turned her onto her side, opened her jaw, bent her knee. Andy seemed disappointed at the failure of his pencil test. Sidelong looks from the staff made him uncomfortable. He had suspected her, held them back, thought she was a fake. He sauntered back to the office.

Mary was opening her other cards now. I looked the other way. Everybody else was still asleep; registration was not until nine on Bank Holidays. Andy got me up anyway.

03

I look at Alison's long auburn hair. 'Do you believe in mermaids, Alison?'

She gives a warm smile. 'Oh yes.'

I look at her eyes, sunk deep into their sockets. 'I am on my way to meet my mermaid, she's taking me to the mer-city.'

'You are mad too, aren't you?' Her face falls.

I feel the raised scars across my throat. 'I'm not mad, I just want to leave this world.' I look at her bandaged wrists. 'And you did too.'

She stares hard at the TV.

'Sorry.' I hug my knees.

'It's okay, I called you mad, didn't I?'

'You bastard!' Clive rubs his bald head, staring at the chessboard. 'You bastard, Ray!'

Ray grins. 'Well, the best man won.' He opens a wooden box by their side and starts to take the pieces off the board.

'Bastard.' Clive gets up and walks out of the day room.

My hot chocolate . . . I pick up the mug, offer it to Alison.

She bites her dry lip. 'No thank you, Wil.' She looks into the mug, shifting, uncomfortable on the floor. 'Wil, do you like the Disney film *Beauty and the Beast*?'

'Yes, yes I do.'

'I have it, if, if you want to watch it with me.'

I take her hand, smiling. 'Okay, I'd like that.'

Staring at my hand holding hers, she pulls away.

'I am sorry.' I look down at my dressing gown. 'I am sorry, I shouldn't have done that.'

'No, it's not you. It's just that nobody does that, it's the way I look, nobody even dares look at me mostly . . .' She stares at the TV as canned laughter spills out from its speaker.

○ℨ

I believed in guardian angels. I thought you could spend your life searching for one, scanning the population for a pair of wings; but you would never find or see anything. Then one day, when you were most in need, when you had lost everything, when you had nobody, one would appear; only you wouldn't notice because they looked, behaved, smelt, felt, like anyone else does. They steadied you through a troubled time where you would have fallen, and then disappeared and you never saw or heard from them again. It was then you knew you'd been touched by a guardian angel.

I believed Beverley was a guardian angel – I was

ninety-nine per cent sure my guess was right. Time would tell. Beverley by my side, we walked round and round the dark concrete courtyard. Without daylight illuminating them, the tall walls round the yard, crusted with broken glass, were backdrops of black. We stopped walking, I rested my head on her shoulder. Tears ran, making my eyes raw. With her thumb, Beverley caressed the back of my bony hand.

'It's all right, Wil,' she whispered. She wrapped her arms around me. I felt the warmth of her arms in the cold air of the night.

We continued to walk round the yard.

That was my first fresh air of the day. Noel did not like me going out. Beverley didn't care what he thought, they had already tried to get rid of her. She thought he was cruel. She got her friends at the nursing agency to continue to book her in here so she could look after me.

Her kids, I knew their lives so well, those children were almost tangible to me. Picturing them from the photo she showed me, getting to know their attitudes from what she told me, it gave me joy. When I heard the fear in her voice as she spoke of the kids' father, who beat her, it made me so angry. I knew she was all right now, now that she had escaped from him. Still it hurt when I listened to the stories she told. Beverley's brown wavy hair, her brown eyes, her manner that only just hid the simmering depression she wouldn't talk about. She cried sometimes, I hugged her and didn't ask questions.

She made me feel tall. Beverley was so small that even in my shrunken state I was taller than her. Fate holds favours for no one, Beverley told me, and it could easily have been one of hers that fell ill. That was why she wouldn't walk away, no matter what they did. I believed her. I believed in guardian angels.

A look halfway between rage and crying filled her eyes when she saw them treating me badly. Her fists clenched around her thumbs as she held back. If I was in seclusion, she took me straight out of there when she came on duty. Officially I was not on a programme, the psychologist Dr Henries had taken me off all behavioural programmes when I came here. That was before Dr Henries left. Now he was gone and no psychologist had taken his place. Still advertising, Pete said. Andy ran things here with a free hand, with nothing written down.

I was rubbing away the tears with my fist as we walked around the courtyard. 'Hush now.' Beverley looked up at me from beneath her fringe. 'Do you want to go in now? I'll make you something to eat.'

'No, thank you,' I mumbled. 'I just want to walk.'

The night air had something special in it. It reminded me of walking on a campsite in the dark: that magical feeling that something strange is out there. If I closed my eyes I could pretend I was not there at all.

Six

Clutching my pillow, I wake suddenly. Cold sweat runs down my forehead. Sleep loosens its grip. I lift my face from the pillow, look at the sunlight flickering on the carpet. My muscles are stiff, sore. I stretch my shoulders back, sit up, twisted in the covers. I prod my damaged hand; dark blotches have soaked through the bandage.

I look into the sunlight shining through the window. The curtains sway, sending shadows across the floor.

Tap, tap. The nurse with the blond bob looks in around the door. 'It's twenty-five past nine, Wil, morning meeting in five minutes.' She takes a step in, smiling.

'I left the clothes your mother brought up with her in the locker – got to go, God knows how many other residents are still in bed!' The door clicks shut again. I hear her knock on the door of the next room. Untangling myself from the sheets, I put my bandaged feet on the floor. The bandages have not come undone . . . I yawn, my hair falls about my face.

Opening the locker, I pull out a pair of jeans and a sweat-top. I sit on the edge of the bed, put on the jeans, the rough denim hard against my legs. I put on the foam slippers, pulling them round the bandages. I push my bad hand carefully through the sleeve of my sweatshirt.

Opening the bedroom door slowly, I look down the corridor. Alison walks past in a thick pink dressing gown and turns the corner. Following her, I stop at the corner and look down the corridor. The office door is open, nurses walking in and out, pushing past Clive as he stands in the doorway.

'Clare, are you going to start or what? I can't hang around all day.' Clive steps into the office.

'Clive, get out!'

Big Mo walks out of the office, looks at me. 'Wil, don't you look drop-dead heaven's-just-walked-by handsome in proper clothes.' He strides down the corridor, puts his arm round my shoulder, leads me up to the day room.

I feel small beside him. I smile.

The armchairs are pulled into a circle, hard plastic seats filling the gaps between them. The TV is off, its black screen reflecting distorted shapes.

Alison sits on a plastic seat on the far side of the circle, her eyes flick away from me uneasily. Clive is resting against the back of the armchair as Ray reads his book, reading over his shoulder. The tall man mutters angrily, staring into his lap on a plastic seat. A man with a shaven head sits cross-legged on an armchair in orange robes.

'Sit next to me, Wil.' Big Mo walks over, pulls out a chair for me as he sits down.

Don't you look drop-dead heaven's-just-walked-by handsome in proper clothes . . . No, I am a freak. No! A freak, a freak . . . I screw my eyes closed. I hear all the patients in the room whispering; he's a freak, a freak . . . I walk over to Mo, sit down next to him. Ray looks up from his book, glances at me. I stare hard at the floor.

'Okay.' The blonde nurse walks in, sits down next to us. 'Let's make a start – Clive, sit down so we can make a start!' She puts her blue folder down on the floor, looks around. 'Okay, anyone with anything particular to chat about this morning?'

'Frank keeps farting.' Clive sits down on the plastic seat next to Ray. 'I am sick of it, Clare, it's bad enough being here without that!' He looks over at Frank slouched in an armchair. 'And he forces them out.' Clive looks down, hiding a smile.

Clare frowns. 'How would you feel, Clive, if someone brought up something like that about you in front of everyone?'

Scratching his bald head, Clive keeps looking at the floor.

'Don't you think you would find it embarrassing?'

Frank burps, gets up out of the armchair, walks through the circle, stops in the doorway, farts and walks out.

Clare puts her thumb against the stud in her nose. I look at Big Mo. I think he wants to laugh.

'See what I mean?' Clive looks around the group.

'Point made, Clive, shall we move on?'

'The kettle's broken.' Ray runs his hand through his hair. 'I haven't been able to make a cup of tea for myself.'

'The toilet stinks of sick, the loo won't flush.' The man in the orange robes looks at the nurse. 'The sick is just in there stinking.'

Alison adjusts her dressing gown.

'How do you feel about that, Tony?'

'Well, it's not very pleasant.' He looks over at Alison. 'However ill someone is, that's no excuse for not cleaning up after they vomit, specially as they always seem to keep themselves clean.'

'Can we change the subject? I know it's not very pleasant, but staff are sorting it with the person involved.' Big Mo grins at Alison. 'If you lot feel you can let it ride for now, it'd be much appreciated.' He smiles, looking about the group. 'I'll make sure maintenance come and fix it.'

The man in the robes uncrosses his legs. I look at Alison.

ය

Joanna wasn't comfortable. She sat down on a seat opposite, her podgy belly bulging beneath her red T-shirt. 'How you doing then on this ward, it's different, isn't it?'

I nodded. Joanna got up, walked over to a cork notice board, read a poster on Mental Health rights. She adjusted her bust, took little notice of the fact that I was watching her. Sitting back on the seat opposite me, Joanna leaned forward, whispered: 'Are you okay?' She stared at me, her brown eyes wide and watery. 'What are they doing to you?' She looked at my thin wasted wrists, arms. Tears blurred my vision, I hung my head. 'Did you hear that Laura died?' Joanna raised her voice.

'What?'

'Laura died.' Brushing the hair from her eyes, Joanna looked at the nurses' station further up the ward.

A telephone rang. A nurse in a white T-shirt, cropped hair, walked out from the back of the station, reached under the counter, answering the phone. He looked down the ward, watching us as he spoke quietly.

'Your hair is growing back.'

I rubbed my hand over my shaved hair, it was not stubble any more.

'You've lost more weight.'

'What, what happened to Laura?'

'She's dead.' Her eyes filled with tears as they fixed on the carpet. 'She went to the hospital last week, Monday. It's fucking Noel's fault! Laura was always vomiting, they were saying she was sticking her fingers down her throat – she kept saying she wasn't but they wouldn't believe her! Then she vomited blood. Maria took her to Casualty and the doctor said she was allergic to wheat products.' Joanna stopped, bit the side of her finger. 'Noel came back on duty that Wednesday – with the rest of the A-shift. He did Morning Points, calling the names from the register. He called for Laura and I said I thought she was being sick in her room and could I go and get her. Noel said no – that it was her responsibility to collect her points on time – and she better not be making herself sick or she would be drinking her Build Up in seclusion. I don't know, Noel must not have been told about what the doctors were saying . . .' Joanna's fingers clenched round her thumbs. She looked up at me, wiping her face with her fist. 'I went to Laura's room after Points, she was lying on the floor – vomit all over the place, blood running from her head, she'd knocked it on the sink. They took her to hospital. She was in a coma all of last week, on Friday she died.' Joanna wiped her eyes again with the back of her fist. She was trembling. She looked up the ward, towards the nurses' station. The nurse in white T-shirt, cropped hair, looked up from his seat behind the counter, stared back at her.

ɕ

'I want, I want to know,' the tall man stops mumbling angrily, sits up in his seat, 'why I am the only gentleman on this unit to have been locked up by you jailer-nurses in that Godforsaken room, on my arrival here three weeks and two days ago.' He stares at Big Mo. 'It was a Thursday, do you remember?' He looks at his watch.

'Do you feel angry about it?' Clare smiles at him.

He runs his hand over his head, it trembles gently.

'The Lord was preaching, yes, preaching through my mortal self – my nakedness was the point of truth and my violence retribution on the sinners of the earth! Like weak-willed servants of the Devil, you silenced me in that bare room!' He looks down at the floor, mumbling to himself.

'Would you rather have been left, Jeff?' Clare's face softens. 'It just seems when you have been left to your torment, with no one to keep you or those around you safe, that distresses you as well. It's not easy for us to know what to do in those situations.' She looks around the group. 'Do any of you have any thoughts?'

ᚷ

Derek was reading *The Times*. His grey beard flecked with black hair, his balding head, forehead creased in concentration. He held a respectability. I envied that. He only got out of seclusion last week but he hid the hurt, dug it deep and denied them the joy of humiliating, breaking. Those were the two things on which they fed: vultures that pecked away at carcases until they were hardly recognizable as their former selves.

Round and round, Derek paced the bare red lino-covered floor fronted by the wide sheet of Perspex. Off Privileges – it and its contents were the first thing everybody saw. Watching Derek in there was like watching a polar bear pace round its pen in the zoo. Round and round the red lino cell he paced. He only banged on the walls on the first and second day, then he quietened down, discovered pacing. He took comfort in their fear, smelling it in that first week of the six that he spent in there, when they only unlocked the door in teams of three, shoving in the dinner tray.

Now he was dressed with no bitter words and a cup of tea by his side and *The Times* in his hands, he sat there in the day area; no dead meat on him for them to feed on. Only a dignity that they could not control.

Ϙ

Clive raises his hand. 'Well, I think all patients like Jeff should be put on an island with a big incinerator and burned and used as fertilizer to feed the rest of us . . .'

'Haven't you got anything fucking useful to say?' Ray looks angrily at Clive. 'You think you're so clever, don't you?'

'Touchy, touchy!' Clive raises his eyebrows, his bald head creases. 'I'm only joking, you know, joke.'

'You're only ever joking.' Ray grabs his book from the floor, gets up. 'Idiot.' He storms out of the day room.

'What's got into him?' Clive looks around the group.

Jeff stands, wringing his hands in the air before him. 'Armageddon, Armageddon, sinners all of you, repent before the fires of Hell!' He grabs the shoulders of the man in the robes. 'Repent, hear the Lord, repent before –'

Knocking the tall man's hands from him, the man in orange robes gets up, walks out of the day room.

'Jeff, chill.' Big Mo walks across, gently tugs the man's sleeve with his large brown hand. 'Don't run with it, don't run with it, this isn't what you want.'

The tall man drops his head, mumbling angrily. Tears stream from his eyes.

'Come on, let's go and have a fag in the smoke room, eh?'

Alison straightens her dressing gown, walks through the circle of chairs.

♋

He was in here before me. It was five in the morning. I was always the one in first, alone in the cell till at least seven. His head was shaved, a red devil tattooed on his neck. He sat on a moulded plastic chair next to the Perspex-covered window. His arm resting on the arm of the chair, 'H-A-T-E' tattooed on his knuckles.

As I paused, Andy pushed me. I stumbled forward, through the doorway, into the red lino-floored cell.

I took my green upright chair from the corner of the room, looking bitterly at the chairs with arms I was not allowed to sit on. I went to the opposite corner of the room, placed my chair in front of the window, sat down to watch the dawn.

The man got up. He staggered forward a few steps, losing his balance. He walked unsteadily towards the observation window. He banged on it, its Perspex bending. 'I know, but, but, but, but, but, but, but, but,' he took a deep breath, 'you fuckin' bastards. I need a, a, a, a, a,' his face turned red, 'I need a fuckin' piss, you fuckin' bastards!'

Andy walked up to the window, turned and walked off down the corridor.

Hammering on the Perspex with his fists, each thud sent it shuddering and bouncing back for more. 'But, but, but, but, but . . .' He picked up a chair, threw it at the window. 'You fu, fu, fu, fu, fu, bastards.' The chair crashed against the Perspex.

Andy did not come back. He knew how maddening patients found that, how to wind them up. He let them freak out, let it teach them a lesson when they realized that their time in solitary had just started again.

The man opened his flies, stumbled towards the chair upturned on the floor. He pissed in a stream of gold all over the chair, then pointed it up at the observation window, pissed over the Perspex. It ran off into a puddle, spreading across the floor. The smell of urine filled the room. I tried not to breathe in, concentrated on the red dawn spreading across the sky.

The door opened. Andy pushed a mop and bucket into the cell.

'Do up your flies.'

'Fu, fu, fu, fu, fuck off!'

The door closed.

'I needed, a fu, fu, fu, piss you bastard.'

The room stank.

'Yes I know, bu, bu, but.' The man stumbled about the cell, to a clean chair, sat down, held his hand out in front of him, looked at the letters on his knuckles. A scar ran across his forehead.

The smell of urine filled my nose. I turned back to the dawn. The darkness was retreating, leaving red, then orange, then clear blue in its wake.

I sat with the man in the smell.

Seven

Sausages, mash and mushy peas. I scrape up the remaining mash and peas with my fork, swallow them down. Taking the plate, I open the door of the bedroom and walk out into the corridor. My foam slippers pat on the carpet. I turn the corner, walk down to the office and knock on the door. I hear chatting on the other side.

The door opens, a nurse smiles at me.

I show her the plate. 'I don't know where the kitchen is.'

She goes back into the office. Big Mo is leaning against the edge of the desk, talking to Clare. Picking up a tray of empty cups, she walks out. 'I'll show you where the kitchen is. My name is Siobhan, we haven't met yet.' The tray clunks as she carries it down the corridor.

'Will you open the door for me?' She stops in front of a door with a window down one side. I push it open, she walks into the kitchen.

'Put your plate in the dishwasher.' She rests the tray on the work surface, switches on a plug and turns on the kettle. 'Your mother – she called, we've put her in the diary to come and visit a week on Thursday. Mo explained that we wanted you to have a little time to settle in.'

Opening the door of the dishwasher, I pull out the rack, slot my plate next to the other dirty dishes.

'Soon you'll be going down to eat with the others in the dining room, it's better not to eat on the ward.' She opens the cupboard above the work surface, takes out a jar of coffee. The kettle begins to steam. 'I think Dr Wilson is coming to see you today.' She spoons the coffee into her mug.

'Nurse, where is the seclusion room, the one the man in the meeting was talking about?'

'You know where your room is?' She puts the coffee back in the cupboard. 'Follow the corridor and it's the last door on the left.' The kettle clicks off, she fills her mug. 'It's not a seclusion room, the door is never locked and a nurse sits outside.' She looks at me, smiling, picks up her mug. 'Now you know where the kitchen is, shall we go back? Clare will be doing your medication.'

She pulls open the door. 'Come on, do you want to take your meds now?'

Meds.

Meds.

She walks out of the kitchen.

Meds.

I hang back, keeping my distance, following her down the corridor.

'Wil, what's wrong?' She turns.

'I'm allergic!' I stop. Big Mo looks around the door of the office. I step back, pressing against the wall.

'If you don't want this medication.' She shrugs her shoulders.

I raise my fists. 'You won't jab me!'

'No, I wasn't saying that.'

'You're not going to jab me!' Big Mo strides down the corridor. My nails dig into the palms of my hands. I stare at Siobhan, holding my fists in front of my face. 'You're not going to jab me!'

Clare hurries after Big Mo, medicine tot in her hand.

'Put your fists down, Wil. Now!'

ભ

It was half past nine. The doctor was choosing. I scratched my fingers down my shaven head, huddling on my plastic upright chair. The room was empty and hollow, the bright lights reflecting off the red lino. I covered my head with my arms, started crying.

I hoped the doctor would choose Lorazepan to sedate me with, at least it had a sleepy-cuddly feeling, like a long-lost call from home, a drifting towards numbness, lights slowly being turned down to dim. What if he gave me Droperidol again? It had me gasping on the floor, locked jaw, muscles in my chest tightening, every breath harder to force, breathing a pitched choking gasp. Teeth locked, my tongue caught between them as they dug into its flesh, I couldn't separate my jaws . . . Jerry would say, 'You get out of that chair one more time and you'll get an injection and you know what that means.' It meant squirming on the floor until the side-effects of the Droperidol wore off, or until Maria came on duty, took pity and injected me with anti-side-effect medication. A Droperidol injection with no side-effect medication, all the staff turning a blind eye to Jerry's punishment . . .

Ann unlocked the door of the cell, walked in, feet echoing on the floor. A medication tot in her hand full of clear fluid.

'I . . . I am allergic to Droperidol.'

She shoved the tot in front of my mouth. I could smell the bitterness.

'How much?' I asked, cringing away.

'Twenty milligrams of Droperidol and five milligrams of side-effect medication if you need it.'

'He hasn't given me enough anti-side-effect medication!' My muscles tightened as I remembered the side-effects.

Elaine walked into the cell and crouched down, wiped away the sweat from the sides of my face as my skin cried.

'We will give you more if you need it.' Ann gave the tot to Elaine. Elaine brought the tot towards my mouth.

'No.'

Elaine looked at the floor, then back at me, bright green eyes . . . 'If you get side-effects, I'll make sure you get the side-effect medication, I promise.'

'The doctor's not prescribed enough, Dr Holding, he prescribes fifteen milligrams because I am allergic – five, it's not enough!' I stared at Elaine. 'It won't do any good.'

Gently she pushed the tot against my lips. 'Wil, it's better than an injection – I've made sure they don't give you an injection before they've given you the chance to take it like this, please.' She brushed her hair from her face. 'Please take it, for me.'

I closed my eyes and swallowed.

ဢ

I put my hands over my ears as I scream. Tucking my elbow into my stomach, I push myself against the wall of the corridor. Droperidol, I know, I know . . . They're not going to jab me! They're not to jab me! I can't breathe, panic swells in my chest, I can't breathe.

'He went like this when I asked him if he wanted his medication.'

'Wil.' Big Mo puts his hand on my shoulder.

'Don't deck me!' I knock his hand from me. 'I'll take it, I am allergic, allergic . . .'

'No one is going to deck you.'

'Don't jab me!' I swing my fists, with my eyes screwed shut.

Big Mo grabs my fists, drawing them together. 'It's okay, Wil.'

The hairs on my neck stand on end. I wait for the floor to slam, crash, smack against my face as they put me down . . .

Big Mo holds down my fists. His hands are warm . . .

I open my eyes, Big Mo a blur in front of me. 'Allergic, allergic . . .'

'Allergic to the medication they gave you?'

I nod, sobbing.

Hollowness fills my chest, my strength leaks out of a hole cut deep inside me.

I pull my hands from his, wrapping my arms around my head. Mother's hug . . . Under the water, the mermaid leads me down, down to the mer-city, holding my hand as she swims with me deep under the sea . . . Mermaid, mermaid! A line of drying blood runs down the cover of the book, down the mermaid beckoning me from the sea . . . I left my book, left it on the bus. I've got to go, go to my mermaid . . .

'We're not going to restrain you.'

I look up at Mo. 'I lost these teeth,' I open my mouth, fingering the gap, 'they broke in one of the spasms.'

I feel the sharpness with my finger. Mother didn't stop them . . . I slide to the floor.

'Why don't you go to your room, have a lie down.'

I look up. Clive and Ray stare at me from the doorway to the day room. Silence rings in my ears.

The mermaid holds my hand. We glide, swimming down, shoals of fish tickle as they swim round us. Towers of seaweed green, the mer-city in the distance below, only the lights in the seaweed towers break the gloom as we dive deeper, away from the sun. I look at the mermaid. She pulls me to her. She smiles, puts her lips to my mouth, kisses me, eating my lip, sucking, biting my tongue. We tumble down through the water, the rough scales of her fin rubbing against me, as she entwines herself between my legs.

Eight

I open my eyes. The sun is shining through the bedroom window. Tangled in the bedsheets, my bad hand in my trousers, bandages twisted round me.

Mermaid . . . I touch my lips with a finger. I close my eyes, turn on my side.

Tap, tap. The bedroom door opens.

'Wil? Dr Wilson wanted to know if you would go down to his office and have a chat with him.'

I roll onto my back.

'Hey, smile.' He grins. 'It's going to be all right. Up, up, up!'

I look at the locker with other people's stickers on

its top. Those people long gone . . . Do they leave only to come back again? Gone . . . Faulty machines not fixed after all, find their stickers still on the locker, nothing changed . . .

I sit up, swing my legs over the edge of the bed. I pull the unravelling bandages from my feet.

'Hey, Wil?'

Throwing the bandages under the bed, I hang my head.

'What are you doing?' Mo sits down, next to me. 'Not all of these places are the same – look at me.' He taps my head gently. 'We want to help you. It won't always be like this; you'll be pulling fit chicks, working, having friends. You need to let someone give you a hand.' He smiles softly. We both look down at the carpet.

Not all hospitals are the same . . . I look at the cuts on my hand, held together by drying scabs.

'I've seen Dr Wilson help a lot of people. Give him a chance?'

'I can't.' I clench my bad hand into a fist, watch the scabs strain across the cuts.

'Are you going to keep your appointment with the doc?' He walks to the door, black pony-tail swinging.

'Yes.' I don't look up.

'Do you want me to walk down with you, or are you all right going on your own?'

'I'm all right.'

The door closes behind him. I stare at my injured hand.

I walk to the end of the corridor and open the doors. The lino is cold on my sore feet. I cross the landing, push open the door to the stairs. Putting my good hand in my trouser pocket, I cross the reception lounge. The receptionist looks up from the semi-circular desk. The doors slide open; I feel the stiff bristles of the doormat under my feet. I step out onto the gravel drive.

'One, two.' I count, pacing myself as I run past the benches, the sores on my feet bleeding from the gravel. Good to bleed. Good to be back to the hard and the cold and the pain . . . I run out through the gates onto the road. I stop, look to my left and right. Which way is seawards? . . . Running, I count, 'One, two, one, two.' Cold wind cuts across my face as cars whoosh past on the road. Stopping, gasping for breath, I look back down the road, towards the hospital. My feet hurt.

I start to run, then turn onto the tree-lined road. Glass shopfronts reflect the clouds. I look up at the sky, clouds tumbling slowly. I lay my palms flat on the glass of a shopfront, squash my nose up against the pane. Hundreds of cards stand in rows around the shop. A girl sits behind a counter at the back, reading a book. My breath mists the window.

Wishing you a Happy Birthday, to the Best Son in the World . . . Tears run down. I wipe them away. I follow the kerb, foot before foot, letting the yellow lines lead.

Houses face each other from either side of the street. Little white-fronted terraces with black doors. A car engine is grumbling, blowing fumes from the other side of the road. A front door slams, and a woman crosses towards the car.

'Miss?'

She turns, looking at me as she reaches the car. Someone inside opens the car door. She pulls her handbag to her.

'Yes?'

A man leans across from the driver's seat, looking at me through the open car door.

'Where is the river?'

'The what?' She rests her hand against the roof.

'The river?'

'Jan!' The man's gruff tone. Clutching her handbag, she tucks her skirt under her legs, gets into the car, slams the door shut. The car pulls out and starts off down the road. I walk after them, my feet sore on the tarmac.

Cars, end to end, smoke and idle around the roundabout, across to the bridge. I walk along the edge of the road, looking into the cars. I breathe the fumes, keeping my bare feet on the yellow line. A little girl puts her open mouth up to the window, looks at me from the back seat. The imprint of her lips left in the misted shape of her breath. I walk past car after car. Two kids in the back of a red one, fighting. Their mother is waving her arms, shouting as I walk past.

Walking away from the road, I cross the grass verge towards a tall red-brick wall. The grass, mushy, is cool under my feet. I jump, grip the top of the wall, pull myself up, the muscles in my arms shaking as my feet struggle to grip against the bricks. Blood from my bad hand collects wet between my fingers. I hold onto the top. I climb up, my sweatshirt catches. As I lie across the wall, the uneven bricks dig into my stomach. I stare down at the green water. Deep dirty swells; the far bank, distant barren factories. I swing my legs onto the wall, sit myself on its edge, feet hanging down above the water. Heavy banks of cloud cover the sky. It is going to rain. Good . . .

The mermaid, is she here?

I look down at the dark moving water.

I kick my feet, letting them bang gently against the bricks. Feel the indent of roughly set cement.

ॐ

A round white cake, bordered by crusted ice waves. The flat white surface had blue icing, a seagull flying next to the words 'Happy 16th Birthday'. I tried to imagine that there were candles burning brightly on the cake, sixteen of them, that hope was still lit up by candlelight. That my seventeenth year had begun with hope, with flame, something to ward off the numbing darkness of these past years.

Andy said to my mum I could not have candles on the cake: fire policy. With something not far from a smile, he told her that although she had not been up for a while she had only half an hour with me. It was Wednesday, a weekday, she should have booked the visit or come at the weekend when visitors were allowed, but as it was my birthday he would make an exception for half an hour.

My cake with no candles of hope for the years ahead. Presents that seemed like empty packages; saying that she wanted to ease the hurt but what could she buy?

I sobbed, burying my head in my arms on the table. Mother asked me if I wanted to cut the cake, but I did not want cake. I wanted to fly like that seagull on the icing in a white sky.

Mother and Father, still not speaking, had both bought me the same present: an electronic organizer. I am supposed to choose which one of them to keep because Mum said it was silly keeping both, 'a waste'. But it was not organizers she was asking me to choose between.

She started to cry. We sat in the corner of the dining room, at the table, watching the minutes as they ticked away. I could hear Brian shouting: 'I want a cigarette, Jack!'

From that dining-room table, two months ago, I escaped and cut my throat. Blood leaked, stained the floor and the walls. Forty-two stitches tried to patch the skin, to stop the flow of blood, to keep life in. Sat here, with my mum, on my birthday, I could cut and cut and cut again until I was dead.

Mum gave me cards from people whose faces I could not picture any more, but who I knew meant something to me a long time ago. I opened the envelopes, reading the messages in the cards one by one. They hoped I was well. How could I be with no candles on my cake? No light to start to scatter the darkness.

Sobs. Sobs that worked up through my gut and blurted in painful spasms, choking me as I cried in front of my mother. Pain that reacted to the presence of a past, of a life I lived, of years where I was a person, not a patient, where my mother was not a visitor but the person my life revolved around.

Andy came to the dining-room door, signalled to my mum. Half an hour was up. Mother hugged me. I did not want to let go. She pushed me away, crying too.

Andy signalled again and Mother walked with Andy out of the dining room. I huddled, covering my head with my hands on the table, shuddering.

❧

'I've seen Dr Wilson help a lot of people. Give him a chance?' I watch the dark water as it drifts past. 'Are you going to keep your appointment with the doc?' My life flickers, I am broken and dead. Carry on, go on in this world where I will never belong, never be human . . . A faulty machine. The river draws my stare, I watch the tumble of the murky, dirty water. I kick my heel against the brick, close my eyes, my fingers rest on the corner of the wall. Mermaid swim up this river, come to me, I need you . . .

I rub my eyes. A plank of wood, one end poking above

the water, covered in slime, drifts downstream. I look across at the factories, barren in the gloom, listening to traffic and the sound of water. I breathe in. The fumes taste bitter. A faulty machine . . .

മ

Sweat. I had been struggling with the nurses on the floor to get the china cup. Three nurses folded me in angled locks. Fighting. Fighting to break the china, leave them only my body. In my mind's eye I saw another broken cup, another deep cut, this time slicing home, the jugular. Andy had had his fun, his nurses were tired, sweating. He told them to hold me still, he pulled down my jeans, sank the fluid between the plunger and the tight sharp needle into my infected potholed bottom.

The Haloperidol was calling, that drugged-up, dosed-up, slip-away feeling. The sleepy-numb, slowsome, brain malfunction sanctuary.

'Take him swimming.' Andy stood at the quiet-room door as the syringe and china cup were taken away. His words created fear, the fear of a doped-up man with a marathon to run. Fear of exhaustion, scared of the aching, the gasping, of the collapse, the rasps for air when they were done with taking me swimming.

I closed my eyes, curled into a ball on the hard concrete floor of the cell.

'Get him up. The others are queuing, waiting to go.'

Picking me up by my arms, the nurses took me through from the cell. A saggy queue stood on the green threadbare carpet before the ward doors.

Skippy, six foot four, with a hanging head. He grinned all the time, loped about gently with a soft grunt that he used to answer everything. Skippy liked it here, they said. Every time they moved him back to a normal hospital, he committed an attack so that he came back. Last time he kicked a nurse in the balls so hard the guy had to have them removed. Once he was here, though, he was the picture of placidity. A gentle giant with a friendly smile.

June, an elderly lady, sixty-something with a leather handbag and thick-rimmed glasses, who always tidied everything, fighting the layers of fag-ash with a disposable cloth. If she did not go to the gym they failed her for 'non-participation' and she went into solitary for a twenty-four-hour target. Some of the nurses felt bad about it. Andy, the charge nurse, said 'The ward programme applies to everybody.'

Andrew slumped against the doorframe, his

beached-whale belly showing. George, Derek and Brian stood holding their hospital hand-out trunks.

Lloyd stepped out of the office, walked over, looked at me kindly with damp eyes. 'You all right?' he whispered.

I shook my head, started crying. The medication was slip-sliding my brain.

Numb, I walked with Lloyd through the grounds on the internal road, past the flowerbeds and lawns that were immaculately shorn and pruned. We passed a bed of crimson Weeping Hearts; it was their time to bloom. The gym and the café at the end of the road, a two-storey red-brick building opposite a cricket pitch. We went down the few wide steps and through the glass double doors to the changing rooms: one for 'Girls', one for 'Boys'. Their metal push-plates and symbols were moist with the condensation that was rolling out over us.

'Who's going in with 'im?' Noel pushed me away from Lloyd, into the changing room.

Heat. The changing room, smelly socks, water that ran around the tiled floor. Boys were in the showers, putting on their clothes or sitting on the wooden benches. George pushed past me, taking off his shirt as he walked up to the bench.

'Okay, hurry up, get changed, out, out into the pool!' the gym instructor shouted. A firm man with small, tight orange trunks. I flinched from his gaze.

'You going in with him, Carl?' Noel asked him.

The gym instructor nodded. 'Get your clothes off, Wil!' His army background snapped loudly in his voice. I could imagine him drilling new recruits in a bullies' paradise. Now he used his skills for the fitness training of disturbed kids. 'Hurry up, hurry up, hurry up! I know your game!' He cocked his head to one side as he watched me undress. 'For every minute you waste it's an extra minute in the water. Hurry up!'

The drugs hurt, my fingers clumsy as they tried to undo the buttons of my top. Carl smiled, pulled at the top I was struggling to take off. It ripped, the tearing of cloth silenced the chatter in the changing room. Only for a second. The noise of washing, farting and voices switched back on.

Noel held my trunks for me to step into. Naked, I stood up, stepped into them. Felt him pull them up round my waist and snap the waistband. The gym instructor pushed me through the de-verruca water onto the white prickle-tile poolside. He grabbed my arm, marched me slowly around to the deep end of the pool.

Yellow indoor kayaks rested against the wall. In an

office built into the space between the pool and the gym hall, the other gym instructor peered at us through the open doorway. He leaned over a folder, twiddling a pen round and round. A ball hammered about in the gym, bouncing, behind shouts and cries and a guy telling someone: 'Fuck you!'

Patients splashed about, the pool walls started to echo with shouts and yells and the noise of breaking water. The gym instructor beckoned Noel with a flick of his hand. Noel stopped leaning on the outside of the viewing bay glass and paced around the pool towards us.

He laid his hand on my shoulder, then pulled my arms behind my back, pinning them, while the gym instructor pulled down my trunks, yanking me out of them in front of the patients and staff.

Pushed, I smacked the water with a slap and a sting of skin.

'Stay away from the sides!' Noel made his way back to the viewing bay. The gym instructor dived in, surfaced and stood, the water lapping around his neck as he steadied himself with his arms. I felt clothed by the water.

Treading water, I stared at the clock on the wall at the far side of the pool. The medication still numbed me, blurred the numbers on the clock. Each swimming session was fifty minutes, but even then it would not end.

He would make me tread water while the others had a Jacuzzi and sauna and then got changed. No standing in the shallow end allowed, just my legs and arms to keep me above the water.

I feared and wanted to drown at the same time. The contradiction was only possible because of my need to rest, rest aching arms and hands, stop kicking against the water. I drifted towards the shallow end, tried to sneak a rest on my toes, to ease my breathing.

The gym instructor dived forward, his hand landing on my head as he pushed me under the water. 'Get back!' I had no time to take a breath, he was holding me under. I opened my eyes, the water stung, I made out the orange colour of his shorts, his legs next to me, his arms pinning me down, holding me underneath. Thrashing about. Need to breathe. Choking. I could feel the veins in my arms rise. He kept holding me under, the water grew hazy. Sensing the growing urgency of my struggling, he let go.

Air. As I thrashed out of the water, he shoved me back into the deep end. Gasping, I stared helplessly at the viewing bay. The clock, a blurred black hand pointed at a right angle, another thirty minutes to go.

સ્જ

'Hey, hey!'

I look down at the grass verge behind me. A little kid stares up at me, hands in his coat pockets. Cars drive past.

Putting his palms on the brick wall above his head, he looks up. His dirty mop of blond hair falling away from his face. 'Can I come up there?'

I turn away, look at the dark water beneath my feet. A submerged plastic bag drifts quickly past.

'Can I come up too? What you doing, what you doing?'

I twist round, look back at the kid. His eyes reflect the banks of clouds. I pick at the loose mortar beneath my fingers.

'Can I climb up there too?'

I look down at the river.

The mermaid rises from the water, her arm reaches out, covered in seaweed. Her wet blond hair sticks to her face, her high pale cheekbones, bright emerald eyes look up as the dark water breaks against her breasts. 'Come, come with me, Wil . . .' The current moves around her.

Big Mo's friendly smile . . .

'Not all of these places are the same – look at me . . . We want to help you. It won't always be like this;

you'll be pulling fit chicks, working, having friends. You need to let someone give you a hand.'

I look down at the young kid as he puts his hands in his coat pockets, walks across the grass to the road. What is he doing out here alone? . . . Cars speed past. Tears fall down my cheek. I wipe them away with my good hand. I look up at the clouds tumbling on themselves in the dull sky. Holding onto the edge of the wall, I pull up my legs, balance, stand up with my arms stretched out like wings, looking down at the river.

The wind buffets against me, blowing hollow sounds, rising, dying away, rising again. I sway on the stone ledge, the wind bites the cuts in my bad hand, bricks dig into my feet. My toes grip to hold my balance.

One easy movement off the wall . . . It starts to rain, I look up at the darkening cloud. The rain hits my cheeks, my nose. I open my mouth, feel the drops prick cool against my closed eyelids. I sway in the wind, listen to the hollow moaning in my ears. Alison's little thin hand in mine . . . Big Mo's broad grin, eyes bright . . . Dr Wilson leans forward, his forehead creases . . . An easy movement off the wall, into the river, into the arms of the mermaid waiting for me . . .

'I've seen Dr Wilson help a lot of people. Give him a chance?' Climb down off the wall, go after the kid, find out what he is doing out here, away from his mum, his dad, his home, his warm room. His mum and dad and sister eating dinner together, him telling them all about his day in school . . .

Tears stream, chased in strange directions on my face by the wind. My arms ache. I let them hang by my sides, stare down at the murky water. 'Come with me, Wil.' Deep under the sea. I feel her lips kiss me.

Stuck in this human world, will I never belong? . . . Alison, tilting her head, smiling nervously, placing her bony fingers against mine . . .

The mermaid reaches out, her skin pale in the dullness. Rain is blowing around, I stand on the wall, numb with cold. She wipes her long strands of hair from her face, bright emerald eyes staring up at me through the dark. 'Are you coming with me?'